The Voyage of the Pegasus

written and illustrated by

Eliza Crooks

"But I expect they had lots of chances, like us, of turning back, only they didn't. And if they had, we shouldn't know, because they'd have been forgotten."

- *J.R.R. Tolkien*

To Mom, Dad, Grammy, Pappy, Evie, and the rest of my family.

Foreword

As a young kid, I loved making stories. I would write and draw pictures on construction paper and staple it all together. I've written chapter books in notebooks too, but I never did finish the longer ones. At the time, it was only a hobby I had found.

I am currently twelve and in the seventh grade. In September of 2021, my literature teacher assigned us to write our own Greek myth, creating our own god or goddess. I showed mine, *The Tale of Maristela*, to my Grammy. She later gave it back to me as a published book for Christmas. That is when I became a true author.

The same year, we dressed up as pirates for Halloween. My big imagination suddenly came up with the idea to write a book about a pirate crew that's made up of unique and quirky kids and their parrot. This time, I actually finished the book. I started out just sketching the five kids: Belle, the brave, reckless, and admired captain of the *Pegasus*, Sydney, an intellectual girl who tends to have quite an attitude, Sawyer, a rambunctious and wild nine-year-old boy, Ryker, a boy who was never wanted as a kid but is adored by his crew, and Alice, a cheerful, energetic, and unpredictable young girl who can master any type of fighting. Then, I began to write.

Although this was a challenging book to write, I am glad to now introduce to you *The Voyage of the Pegasus.*

Table of Contents

CHAPTER	PAGE

The Stowaways

It was the year of 1693 when I, Belle Smith, became the captain of the *Pegasus*. I was twelve years old at that time. I had been living on a pirate ship, the *Cobra*, all my life with a band of ruthless pirates and their captain, Clark Teach. My only dream was to leave.

It was a big ship. We had gold, precious stones, and everything you could ever want. I did not appreciate it, though. How could I? This crew, just like every other, was terrible and murderous.

My parents were never a part of this story, because they died when I was only two. That left me with the captain. He was cruel to me. I thought I'd learned to deal with it. The only problem was I didn't. I couldn't. Everyone was just cruel.

So, I ran away. It was easier than I thought it would be. The rest of the crew was strangely distracted. I simply got in one of our rowboats in the middle of the night. Then I rowed to the nearest island and spent the night there. I woke up the next morning, and the ship was gone. Those wretched, cruel pirates were gone. I was on my own. I searched the island for treasure, food, civilization, or anything. I couldn't believe it when I found an abandoned pirate ship.

I fixed it up just enough to make it sail properly. It was smaller than the *Cobra*, but far more beautiful, and it seemed as though I knew this ship, from a long, long time ago. The ship and everything in it was mine. I had just become the captain of the *Pegasus*.

Now the only thing I didn't have was a crew. I did need one. But I wanted my crew to be different from the one I had been with before. Eventually I had one, and they were just the kinds of people I wanted on my ship. Even better, they were all kids. None of them intended to be on the *Pegasus*, but we just happened to find each other.

First was Sydney Andrews, who had light brown hair and pretty brown eyes. She was so smart that her parents sent her off to a special boarding school when she was eleven years old. However, the teachers were harsh and the schoolgirls bullied her and she grew tired of it. So, when she was thirteen years old, she realized she was on her own and ran away. She later found herself lost, broke, and alone in a harbor.

The harbor she was in just so happened to be one I sailed to. Seeing her crying and alone, I assumed she was a runaway. So, I decided to ask her if she wanted to start a pirate crew with me. It was a silly question, but Sydney was absolutely desperate at that time. She told me all about what had happened and decided to come with me on the *Pegasus*.

Sydney was a strange girl, or strange to me, at least. She worried about everything and hated taking risks of any kind. I didn't see how she could possibly come with me, but she did, and I was glad.

About a week later, a terrible storm hit at sea. We soon saw a young boy floating on a crate, who looked like he couldn't hold on any longer. Before we could throw him a rope, he had passed out.

Sydney was terrified and didn't know what to do. So, I jumped off of the ship and plunged into the water. Somehow, I just barely made it up above the water again. I struggled to swim to the boy, and I soon reached the crate as Sydney threw a rope towards me. It smacked me in the face, but I was able to grab it as Sydney pulled us to the ship. After that, we were all safe.

We later found out that the boy's name was Sawyer Anderson. He was eight years old with curly brown hair that he had stuffed into a hat and bright blue eyes. His mother had died of the influenza. His father was a fisherman from Massachusetts and was on his boat with Sawyer during the storm. Sawyer had fallen off, landed on an old storage crate, and had drifted toward the *Pegasus* just in time for Sydney and me to save him.

Next came Ryker Collins, a boy with dark and deep brown eyes and brown hair. His parents divorced when he was very young, so he never knew his mother. He and his father were very rich. When he was twelve years old, they went on a business trip to the harbor in London. He got lost and wound up running from two ugly bandits.

By sheer coincidence, we were on that beach. So, Ryker hopped on the *Pegasus* and refused to go back. There was something about him… something I couldn't understand but liked. There was something I saw in him that I had never seen, but I didn't know what it was.

Alice Williams was the last kid to join our crew. She was a girl with vibrant red hair who lived at an orphanage in Salem and hated it. At six years old, she decided to run away. So, one night she climbed out of the window and wandered away to the shore. The *Pegasus* had crashed on the same shore during a storm. Alice found her way into the ship and we decided to let her stay.

Now, all we needed was a crew name. It took us hours to come up with one. Alice was hanging upside down, Sawyer had food all over his face, Sydney had her nose buried in a dictionary, and Ryker had fallen asleep. I just sat there, thinking.

"Stowaways," Sydney said.

"That's the silliest thing I've ever heard." Ryker had just woken up.

"How did you hear that?" Sydney asked.

"I was listening to you in my sleep. I had the most wonderful dream. I met a beautiful girl with bright green eyes and golden hair."

"Wait a minute," Sawyer interrupted. "You're not describing…"

"What's a stowaway?" Alice asked.

"A dumb name for our crew," Ryker answered.

"No, look." Sydney said. "Another word for stowaway is a runaway, and me, Alice, and Belle are all runaways."

"I like the name," I commented.

"Give me that." Ryker snatched the dictionary and looked inside. "We didn't sneak on a ship and try not to be seen."

"That's not the point. It's a good name." Sydney said. "All in favor say 'aye'."

We all agreed, except for Ryker. Just then, a parrot swooped down and hit the back of Ryker's head.

"Aye-aye, Captain!" she squawked. "Stowaways!"

"Stowaways it is!" I exclaimed.

As for the parrot, she ended up living with us. We named her Donna and she proved to be both amazing and also very annoying. But she was still a great member of the crew. And so, the Stowaways came to be in the year of 1693.

The Legend of Lost Island

A year had passed and it was now May of 1694. I had just turned thirteen. However, we had begun to get bored of doing the same things over and over again. Though we did not notice it at first, we had begun to form our own routine. We needed a change.

One day, when we were all sitting down and doing nothing, Alice brought up our problem.

"Are we ever going to do something fun?" she asked.

"What do you mean?" Sydney asked her.

"We always do the same thing every day and I'm bored," she said.

"Yeah, Belle." Ryker interjected. "Even Donna agrees."

"*Squawk!* Bored! No fun!" Donna complained. "Bad Captain! Bad Captain!"

"Stop it, Donna," I said.

"Mean Captain! *Squawk!*" Donna flew below deck repeating, "Mean Captain!"

I rolled my eyes.

"You're the boring-est captain ever," Sawyer complained.

"We have a few more treasure maps below deck," Sydney said.

"But we already have treasure," Alice whined.

"Yeah, Sydney, your idea is dumb," Ryker said.
"I want a challenge!" Sawyer exclaimed. "I want to wrestle a shark!"

Ryker stared at Sawyer. "Why would you… you know what, I'm not even gonna ask. It doesn't involve me and I really don't care."
"You could practice your sword fighting," Sydney suggested.

"No! No! No!" Sawyer complained.

I tuned out their bickering and tried to think. Then it hit me.

"Guys! Guys! Be quiet!" I hushed them. "Have you ever heard of the Legend of Lost Island?"

"I don't want a story," Sawyer grumbled.

"Just listen," I said. "It's a treasure hunt we could do."

"But we *have* treasure," Alice repeated.

"Yeah, but Belle's ideas are actually good," Ryker said.

"No. It's not about the treasure. The journey is almost impossible." I said. "Just listen."

Everyone quieted down and got ready to hear about the legend. The word 'impossible' had caught their attention.

"So," I said, "They say there's an island that holds tons and tons of treasure. The thing is, no one is really sure where it is, but I might know where the map may be. One time, my old captain and his crew went down to an old shop by the seaside. He wanted the map to Lost Island and dropped a huge bag of gold on the ground. The old salesman wanted forty-nine more and turned my captain down because he wasn't willing to give any more. I remember the bag weighed fifty pounds."

"Fifty bags, each one is fifty pounds." Sydney figured. "We need two thousand five hundred pounds of gold. We can do that."

"Yes. I also think I have a map to get to the shop. So, we can get to the shop and get the map and go to the island, but Lost Island is said to be one of the most dangerous places in the world. You see, the island is surrounded by shallow, rapid water. The only way we could get to the island is to leave the *Pegasus* at sea and use the rocks surrounding it.

"Once we get to the island, there will be poisonous centipedes, spiders, and snakes, other things like quicksand and geysers. Once we get to the center of Lost Island, we have to find a trapdoor and go underground. Then, there will be traps and obstacles until we get to the key. Once we get the key, we climb a ladder through a mountain until we are above ground.

Then, we climb to the top of the mountain, dig up the treasure, and carry the chest back to the *Pegasus*. This is all if that man even has the map, and if Lost Island is even real." I finished. "Does that sound easy enough?"

"Yes! Yes! Yes! See Sydney, all of Belle's ideas are better than yours!" Ryker exclaimed.

"No!" Sydney argued. "Not in a million years! Never will I face quicksand, poisonous bugs, traps…"

"All in favor say 'aye'." I interrupted.

"Aye!"

"Majority wins!" I exclaimed.

Everyone, except for Sydney, rushed to the storage room to find the map. I found it in one of my old chests and handed it to Ryker. He and I would always steer the ship. It just seemed boring for one person to have to stay out there all alone.

"You want to go to Seaside Scalawags? That's so small I can't even tell if it's on this map." Ryker said.

I studied it, then said, "That's the store that had the map. Come on." I walked toward the front of the boat.

We were about to go on the journey of our lives.

Captain For a Night

We had been sailing for a few days and finally arrived at the shop.

We planned to put all fifty bags of gold on the shore. Then, Ryker and I would go ask the man for the map. After that, the three of us would come back to the shore to get the gold. We would take it to the shop, get the map, and come back to the ship to sail off.

We would have to take many trips, so this whole plan would probably take hours, and I did not want to leave Sawyer and Alice alone that long. Sydney was usually organized and on top of things, so I put her in charge.

As Ryker and I left the ship, Alice shouted, "Why can't we come?"

"Pirates can be dangerous." I said. "If a fight breaks out, I don't want you to be a part of it."

"That's not fair!" Alice argued.

"Yeah!" Sawyer exclaimed. "We can fight, too!" He made fists and tried to look tough. He didn't look tough, though. In fact, it was a hilarious sight to see.

"Well," Alice asked, "what about Sydney? She's fourteen."

"She needs to look after you," I said.

"We can look after ourselves!" Sawyer shouted.

"We want independence!" Alice exclaimed.

"Independence!" the two of them shouted. "Independence! Independence! Independence! In…"
"Okay! Stop it!" I cried. "We have to go. Don't get into any trouble!"

Ryker and I walked away from the *Pegasus*. I gripped my sword and worried about what might happen to us and the others on the ship.

We did our business with the salesman and everything went well. Meanwhile, things were not going so well for Sydney.

Sawyer and Alice were up to no good. As they had said before, they wanted 'independence'. So, the two began to plot against Sydney. Meanwhile, Sydney was pacing back and forth trying to come up with a plan to look after two uncontrollable kids.

At dinner, the three were eating a nice meal of mashed potatoes with gravy and steak. Sydney was so stressed out that she didn't see Sawyer and Alice getting ready to do something she would absolutely hate.

Alice took a pebble and put it on the table. She then took a spoonful of gravy and set the spoon on top of the pebble, with the gravy facing herself. She winked at Sawyer. He took his fist and smashed it on the end of the spoon. The gravy went flying toward Sydney, leaving a big smudge on her white blouse!

Sydney was furious.

"Alice!" Sydney screamed. "Do you know how much this blouse cost? It's from Great Britain and it's irreplaceable!"

Alice began to cry and said, "You don't have to be so mean, Sydney. You hurt my feelings!"

"Stop whining!" Sydney shouted. "I knew this would happen. Shame on you, Alice! And you, too, Sawyer! You know better than this!"

Sydney stormed off into her bedroom. As she searched her dresser trying to find a blouse, she felt the *Pegasus* make a sudden movement. She dashed out of the room and couldn't believe her eyes. She saw Sawyer standing at the steering wheel and Alice hanging off of a rope with every sail hoisted.

"What have you done?" she screamed at the top of her lungs.

She stood there, frozen in horror. A storm was going on inside her. She felt as though she could hear the thunder that was raging in her mind. Only that thunder wasn't coming from her. A real storm was taking place on the water!

Sawyer lost his grip on the steering wheel and fell. The *Pegasus* veered back and forth, up and down. It felt like an earthquake rather than a storm. Sawyer looked around and began to cry.

Alice began to cry, too. She clung to the rope she was on. She could not get down.

Sydney realized that the wind and waves would tip the *Pegasus* over.

"Alice," she cried, "do something about the sails!"

"I don't know what to do!" Alice screamed.

Sydney had no idea what to do, and she didn't want to make Sawyer do anything. So, she went below deck to get Donna. Maybe, she somehow magically knew what to do, but Donna was nowhere to be seen. Sydney felt hopeless but she had no time for that. She knew Sawyer and Alice were her responsibility and she knew she had to do something.

So, she did something reckless. She grabbed a sword and ran to the upper deck. She held the sword with her teeth and began to climb. When she reached the sails, she held onto the pole with her legs and slashed the sail down the middle. She climbed higher, ripping and tearing at the sails so that they did not catch the wind anymore.

She climbed over to the rope Alice was on. Just then, the rope untied itself and gave way. Sydney grabbed Alice. She hung onto a beam with her feet.

"Sawyer!" Sydney cried. "Get every bag of flour we have and make a pile!"

Eventually, there was a big soft pile of flour beneath the two.

"Alice!" Sydney shouted, "I'm going to let go! On three. One, two, three!"

Sydney let go and Alice fell. Thankfully, she did land on the flour. She was safe. Sydney let go of the beam and landed on the flour.

"Come on," she said. "Let's go to my bedroom."

When they were all in Sydney's bedroom, Sawyer burst into tears.

"What's wrong?" Alice asked as she tried to comfort him.

"I don't want to talk about it," Sawyer said.

Sydney knew. That storm was just like the one that took place the night Sawyer had been separated from his father and had almost died. His dad was the most important person in the world to him. Everyone had thought he had gotten over it. Sydney dried Sawyer's eyes and put the two children to bed. They fell asleep quickly, but Sydney stayed up until the storm was over.

In the morning, the three got in an escape boat and rowed to the shore. They took a bag of gold with them.

Ryker and I had the map and had been sitting on the shore all night. We saw Sydney and the others pull up to the shore in a rowboat with a bag of gold. They walked past us and into the shop. We watched them come out with new sails.

"So," I said awkwardly. "How did you like being captain for a night?"

"Never again!" Sydney declared.

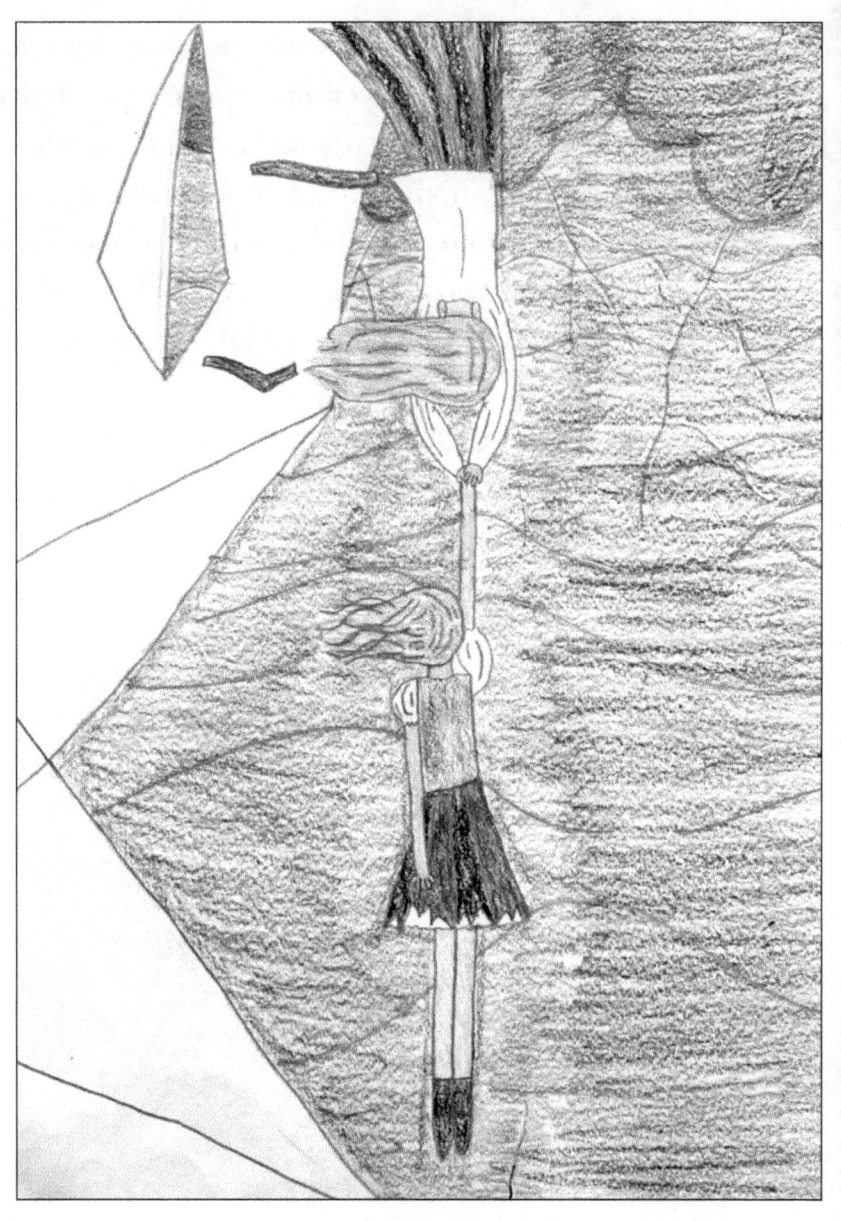

Shark Island

We were making progress. The sails were fixed and we were on our way to Lost Island.

"Hey, Belle!" Sawyer jumped up and down pointing at a small island. "Can we go to that island?"

I looked at the map. The island didn't even have a name.

"Why?" I asked.

"I'm pretty sure there's a reason nobody lives there." Sydney said, "Oh! I bet it's one of those islands that's surrounded by sharks! I read about one of those!"

"You can't believe everything you read in books," I said.

"I don't, but this is real. There's a reason no one lives there."

"She does have a point, Sawyer," I said.

"Oh, come on," Sawyer said. "The ship's drifting toward it anyway. Can we not just take a look?"

"No," I said.

"I'll give you my spyglass."

Now I had to say "yes". Of all of the things on this ship, Sawyer's spyglass was the one thing I longed to have and Sawyer knew it.

"Ugh. Fine"

"Yay! Can I steer?"

"No."

I began to follow the map to the strange island Sawyer wanted to go to so badly. He seemed to know something about it that intrigued him to go there, something I wouldn't like. My gut was telling me to go back, but I didn't want to upset Sawyer, not to mention getting that nice spyglass! Plus, a little excitement wouldn't hurt.

We approached the island, and Ryker walked onto the deck. He looked confused, but then frightened, and then angry. He turned toward me.

"Belle!" he shouted. "What do you think you're doing!"

My face turned red-hot. I had just realized that I was leading the *Pegasus* into a disaster waiting to happen. I did not answer.

"Belle, you can't take us here. The water's infested with sharks!" Ryker shouted.

"No, it's not," I lied. "Not everything Sydney reads is true, you know that."

"This island is famous for its sharks. Fishermen talk about it all the time; pirates, too. What were you thinking?"

Sawyer knew about the sharks. Just then it all came together. I remembered the folk tales and stories my old crew told. I remembered listening so intently as I washed every dish that had been used that night. I remembered the horror the day we came upon that island... the day we were attacked by massive sharks.

Tears began to form in my eyes. "But why would Sawyer want to be here?" I wondered.

"I just forgot! I didn't mean to make you hate me!" I was sobbing. "I didn't mean to put us all in danger! I didn't think Sawyer would want to take us here!"

I hated the idea of putting my crew in danger. "Good captains are better than this," I thought.

"Belle! Stop whining and get this ship turned around!"

"It's too late," I said, shaking my head.

"Yeah! Now that you've wasted all your time crying!"

"I'm sorry if I'm just not good enough for you, and I'm sorry if…"

A fifteen-foot-long shark jumped up out of the water, followed by another, and another!

"I'm gonna wrestle a shark!" Sawyer exclaimed.

"Sawyer, no!" I ran after him. I didn't know what to do. The only thing I could manage was to sit there and cry over the entire situation. But I couldn't do that. I couldn't do that because I was stronger than that. I had to save him.

Then I stopped. There were hundreds of sharks surrounding the *Pegasus*! We were trapped!

"Ryker!" I shouted. "Try to clear a pathway for the *Pegasus*. Sydney, I want you to steer. Alice, when I say 'go' I want you to pull that rope as quickly as you possibly can."

They all went to their places. I had no idea whether this would work or not, but this was our only option. Rescuing Sawyer was up to me.

"He seems to be having a good time." I thought. "Lucky for me, he picked the biggest shark in the sea! What a great day I'm having! Ryker hates me, I put my crew in danger, and Sawyer is wrestling a shark! Ugh."

As I ran I remembered the night I met Sawyer, the night I did something reckless and crazy to save him. I had to do the same now.

I stood on the rail of the ship. I held tight to my sword, brushed my hair back, took a deep breath, and jumped.

The moment my feet left that rail I thought would surely die. To my relief, I didn't!

I was standing on a shark. It felt me on its back, and it flew into a rage! It began to twirl and jump and completely lose control! I was going to slip and fall into the water filled with sharks that would eat me alive!

I jammed my sword into the shark's back. It became even angrier! I knew it would do something crazy, so I pulled my sword out, and just then it threw me into the air!

I flew up, and as I fell I realized I was headed straight for the shark's mouth! I held my sword out to the side and dived headfirst. Just before my head reached its mouth, I slashed my sword straight down the shark's nose. I landed and ran down the shark's back and jumped.

I landed on another shark, but this one didn't notice me. I quickly ran across its back before it could attack. I jumped and landed on the shark Sawyer was fighting. He was sword fighting, not wrestling, but that didn't matter. This shark was very, very angry. I didn't know how Sawyer had lasted this long, but he wouldn't last much longer.

Just like the other shark, it threw us into the air. Sawyer fell right into the shark's mouth! I fell in and jammed my sword in its mouth, keeping it open.

The shark was tossing and turning, and swallowed Sawyer's sword! The shark was unconscious and began to sink! It was going head first, so it would have been easy to slip out.

"Sawyer!" I shouted. "Come on!"

"But my sword is down there!"

"Sawyer, we don't have time for that! If my sword gets knocked out, the shark's mouth will be closed for good and we'll be trapped!" I tried to talk fast and not waste any time, but Sawyer didn't understand the problem. When water began to rush into the shark's mouth, I knew we were in trouble.

"Come on!" I screamed. I yanked Sawyer's hand and tried to shove him out, but before I could, the inside of the shark filled up with darkness. We were trapped!

I didn't know why, but I found I had matches in my pocket. I lit one and looked around. The water was already two feet deep!

"No way!" Sawyer exclaimed. "You lit a fire inside a shark's stomach! Awesome!"

"Sawyer!" I cried. "Help me!"

I was pushing up on the roof of the mouth with one hand and holding the match with the other. Even after Sawyer came to help, it wouldn't open.

The water kept on seeping through the gaps in the teeth. I tried and tried and the water grew higher and higher. I thought, "Belle, look what you've done! You and Sawyer are going to die and surely Ryker is already dead and Alice and Sydney know nothing about ships. This is the end of the Stowaways! Oh, be quiet, Belle. You know you're not going to die!"

I didn't think things could get any worse when I saw that the water was up to my shoulders. It was no use to keep trying to push on the mouth. I truly thought I would die.

"Belle," Sawyer said softly with tears in his eyes. "It's too late. I'm sorry for getting you into this. It's all my fault, and if we make it don't let the crew tell you otherwise. I knew about this island and knew you'd forget and I knew everyone would blame you. If we make it, you can kick me out. I'll even walk the plank. You can hate me all you want to."

I smiled softly and said, "I will never hate you. You're like a little brother to me, and I promise you, we will make it out of here. Also, we don't have a plank. Whoa!"

I slipped and my foot hit one of the shark's teeth. The match went out. Just then the water flew in faster than before! Then I knew how to save us! I stood up.

"Sawyer, the teeth!" I shouted, just before the water completely took over the shark's mouth.

We both felt for the teeth and began to kick and push them out. After a minute there was a hole for us to swim out of. I climbed through and helped Sawyer out. We both quickly swam up and gasped for air.

The sharks didn't care much for us, but we swam quickly, knowing that the unconscious shark would wake up any minute. There was an emergency rope hanging off of the left side of the *Pegasus*. We climbed up onto the ship. I looked around at the others.

"Go!" I shouted.

The sails went up and the ship moved away from the island. Ryker, who was still fighting off the sharks, grabbed the emergency rope and climbed into the ship.

I looked at Sawyer and exclaimed, "We're alive!"

"I know! We're alive!"

We rejoiced and jumped around happily. But then Ryker walked up.

I couldn't bear to look at him or talk to him. I ran into my room and locked myself inside.

Tell Me

I had been in my room for hours, crying the whole time. I had changed into clean clothes and now I was just sobbing at my desk. Then, I heard a knock on the door.

"Belle, please let me in! Please! You can talk to me! Come on. Talking always makes me feel better."

It was Sydney.

"Sydney, please. Just leave." I said. "I need some time alone."

"You've had time alone."

I saw a knife slide through the crack in the door and pull the lock up. Sydney walked in. She sat on the hammock.

"So, tell me what's up. Look, you're not a bad captain, and you're not a failure! It was all Sawyer's fault. He tricked you! And I'm sure Ryker doesn't hate you, he's just a jerk like most boys his age. Even if…"

"Sydney, please. Stop trying to make things better." I pleaded. "You don't get it. It's not about Sawyer, and I know I'm a decent captain."

"That's it!" Sydney exclaimed. "You've been thinking you're not good enough for a long time, haven't you?"

"Well…"

"And then what happened today got you all emotional and…"

She just went on and on about this situation she thought I was in. She still didn't get it really. I did feel like I wasn't good enough, but Sydney didn't actually know what was wrong.

"Sydney, look. I know I'm a good captain, okay?" I interrupted. "I just don't know if… someone else does."

"Who?"

My face turned bright red. If I told Sydney this, I would be more embarrassed than I ever have been.

"It's Ryker, isn't it?" Sydney exclaimed.

My face became even redder. I was busted.

"Oh! You like Ryker!" Sydney giggled.

"So what if I do?"

"Tell me if I'm right. You like Ryker, and you've been trying to win his approval. Then, he got mad at you when you already felt insecure. So, now you feel like you'll never win his approval and also never get over him. Now, is that right?"

I stood there, shocked at Sydney's figuring this out and not knowing what to say.

"Well," I started. "Oh, I can't tell you this."

"Why not?" Sydney asked.

"It's embarrassing."
"Tell me!"

"No," I argued.

"Tell me! Oh, please! Please tell me!" Sydney begged.

"Fine." I said. "It's… not *like*."

"What do you mean?" Sydney looked confused.

"I mean I don't *like* Ryker, I…"

"You what?" Sydney asked.

"Please don't laugh at me," I said. "You know what love at first sight is, don't you?"

"Belle, you can't… no… you… but that's not fair! Your love is right there and mine is a noble in London. You're only thirteen and why Ryker? He's not even cute. Maybe you need eyeglasses!"

"No, Sydney." I interrupted. "Ever since the first time I saw his face I knew he was perfect, but it's almost impossible for him to love me back."

"Well," Sydney said, "getting the treasure from Lost Island is almost impossible, but we're doing it, so maybe Ryker *is* in love with you."

Meanwhile, Ryker was laying in his hammock and staring at the wall. Sawyer knocked on the door.

"Go away, Sawyer," Ryker yelled through the door.

Sawyer would not leave, "But Ryker…"

"Go away, Sawyer," Ryker repeated flatly.

"Now, Ryker," Sawyer said, "don't you hate it when Belle's right?"

"No," Ryker said.

"What about Sydney?"

"Sure."

"Remember that time she said that all boys your age are immature?"

"Yeah."

"Well, I guess you're one of them."

"One of what?" Ryker asked.

"The immature boys your age."

"Oh."

"Don't you want to prove her wrong?"

"I guess..."

"Well, it's not very mature to sit there and stare at a wall instead of talking to your fellow friend when you're having an emotional breakdown." Sawyer said. "So I suggest you let me in."

"How did you know I was staring at the wall?" Ryker demanded.

"That doesn't matter. What does matter is that you're a mess and I'm here to fix you, don't you agree?" Sawyer knew this would get Ryker to open the door.

"Yeah," Ryker said blankly.

"Great, now let me in."

Sawyer had outsmarted Ryker. Ryker opened the door. He looked absolutely depressed.

"Alright, young patient!" Sawyer exclaimed. "Are you mentally ill?"

"I don't think so," Ryker said doubtfully.

"Did you catch a cold?"

"No."

"Do you have influenza?"

"Sawyer!" Ryker yelled. "I'm not sick!"

"Have you been dealing with skin problems, such as leprosy or mosquito bites?"

"No!" Ryker screamed.

"Do you have any heart issues?" Sawyer asked.

"Sawyer, that's it," Ryker said, even more depressed. "It's broken."

"But I can only fix broken bones," Sawyer said.

"No, Sawyer. It's not *actually* broken."

"You lied!"

"No, Sawyer. It's just something you say when you're really sad because the girl of your dreams hates you and you feel like your life is over."

"Why does Belle hate you?" Sawyer inquired.

"Because she... Wait. How did you know it was Belle?"

"Just answer the question," Sawyer said.

"Because I made her think she's not good enough for me and now she may never speak to me again," Ryker sighed.

"So, are you in love with Belle?" Sawyer asked.

"Yep," Ryker admitted.

"Ryker, you do not have heart problems, you are mentally ill," Sawyer proclaimed.

The whole time Alice had been spying on the two groups. She was the only one who knew that Ryker and I were in love with each other.

The next night after dinner Alice called Sawyer and Sydney.

"So," Alice whispered, "Ryker loves Belle."

Sydney smiled with excitement.

"And Belle loves Ryker," Alice whispered and giggled a little.

"So?" Sawyer shrugged. "What does that have to do with anything?"

"Do you know nothing?" Sydney whispered. "If they both dream of the other person loving them, then both of their dreams have come true! Don't you get it? They were meant for each other! This is amazing! Wait, Alice... how do you know all of this?"

"I was spying," Alice grinned.

"So they're both psychos?" Sawyer asked.

"No," Sydney shook her head and gave Sawyer a look.

"This is great!" Alice exclaimed. "We have to tell them!"

"No, Alice, that's not how it works," Sydney said. "Oh, whatever."

They called us saying they had good news and we both came, but before they could say anything a thought popped into my mind.

"Wait, guys," I said. "When was the last time we saw Donna?"

Where's Donna?

"Is that really important?" Sawyer complained.

"Yes," I said. "I haven't seen her since we left Seaside Scalawags."

"Oh no!" Alice said with a concerned look on her face. "Is she lost?"

"No," Ryker reassured her. "That was only a few days ago. I'm sure she's just hiding."

"I know Donna," I said. "She doesn't just hide. There must be a reason she's disappeared."

"Do you think she flew away when you yelled at her, you know, before you told us about Lost Island?" Sydney asked.

"No," I replied. "I saw her after that."

"What about during the storm?" Sawyer asked.

"Birds don't like to fly in the rain," Sydney argued.

"Did she fly away yesterday because she didn't like the sharks?" Alice asked.

"She wouldn't fly away, she would hide," Sydney insisted.

"Wait. That only happened yesterday," I said. "She's probably still hiding!"

We turned the *Pegasus* inside out and searched everywhere, but after seven hours of making no progress, we decided Donna was not on the ship. We couldn't lure her out and she didn't come when we called. It was two o'clock in the morning, and we all had to go to bed. I didn't sleep, though.

I felt like I had to be this awesome person who did everything right, but no matter what I did or how hard I tried, everything just went wrong. We had barely covered any of this journey, and we had already had enough problems.

I almost wanted to not go to Lost Island, knowing how much trouble it would be. But then I made up my mind to go. I decided if we could fight off sharks that were fifteen feet long, and do anything else we've done on previous adventures, then we could go to Lost Island.

The next morning the first thing we did was talk about Donna.

"I'm too tired to think," Alice complained.

I was, too.

"Alice," I said, "you can go. Sawyer, you, too. You need to get some rest."

They both left and went to their rooms.

Sydney, Ryker, and I sat there and tried to think, but nothing worked. Every idea we came up with wouldn't have been right. I had almost lost hope when a decent idea came to my mind.

"Do parrots like to be with their families?" I asked.

"Yes," Sydney said. "Last night I couldn't sleep, so I read a book about parrots to get ideas. It said they live in flocks, which means Donna is probably with other parrots."

"Donna doesn't like to fly far. Let me see if there is anywhere close to Seaside Scalawags she could have gone to."

I looked at the map. There was an island only four miles away from the shop named Parrot Island. It must be where she had gone!

"I think she went to Parrot Island!" I exclaimed. I handed the map to Ryker.

"But what if she's not there?" Ryker argued. "We would have wasted a lot of time. Also, the only way to get there it looks like is to go through this passage, but it's filled with robbers and bandits."

I looked at the map. It was true. It was either bandits, whirlpools, rapids, or huge rocks. The whirlpools and rapids would sink the *Pegasus,* and the rocks were like a high and jagged wall to keep us out.

"Let me see," Sydney begged.

Ryker handed Sydney the map.

"I say we try to fight off the bandits if that means we can get Donna," she said.

"You won't listen," Ryker disagreed. "We may risk our lives for no reason."

"But what if she is there? Are you just going to leave her?" Sydney argued.

"No," Ryker answered. "I'm just saying we should be a bit smarter making descisions when it comes to bandits."

"Who cares about bandits?" Sydney scoffed.

"Me!" Ryker shouted.

"Why?" Sydney asked rudely. "Are you afraid of bandits?"

I watched the two bicker. I didn't want to make one of the two upset, but if we didn't try anything we could to get Donna back, we would all be devastated. I knew Ryker didn't want to do this only because of the bandits he was running from when we met him, but that was over. If he was going to be a pirate, he had to get over it. Donna was too important to let go of.

That night while all five of us were sitting at the table I came to a decision.

"Everyone," I got their attention. "I know how we can get Donna… maybe. She's most likely on an island south of Seaside Scalawags called Parrot Island." I pointed to the map. "Now," I said, "the only way to get to Parrot Island is to go through this passage. The problem with that is that the passage is filled with bandits and outlaws. We…"

"Belle," Sawyer interjected. "Going through that passage is a very stupid idea, and I should know because I'm the smartest. Plus…"

"Sawyer," Sydney interrupted," you're the…"

"Shush," Sawyer continued, "As I was saying before *someone* interrupted me, ec-hec-hem…"

"What's that supposed to mean?" Ryker asked.

"I was clearing my throat," Sawyer answered.

"That's not how you clear your throat!" Alice argued. "Watch."

She started making annoying coughing noises.

"Can I just say what I was going to say?" Sydney tried to yell over Alice.

"No!" Sawyer yelled back.

"I was trying to say that you're not the smartest! You're the dumbest!" Sydney shouted.

"No!" Sawyer bellowed. "You are!"

"Guys! Stop it!" I tried to scream over them.

I tried and tried to get them to be quiet until Ryker finally suggested that we tie them up.

So I did. When I was done, Sawyer, Alice, and Sydney all sat on the sofa... strangely enough we did have a sofa... with their hands tied behind them and their ankles crisscrossed and tied together. Their mouths had been gagged, too. I could finally think straight and sighed with relief. We had things to take care of, so I freed them and the chatter began to rise up again.

"Belle, why did you have to do that?" Sawyer complained.

"To get *you* to shut up," Ryker said.

"Ryker! You don't need to say that in front of Sawyer and Alice! They still have very young ears!" Sydney scolded.

"Well, how was I supposed to know? They're pirates, aren't they? They're not chickens like you are," Ryker teased.

"Chicken! I'm not a…"

"Okay! Okay!" I interrupted. "This is the part where everyone is quiet so that we can hear our own thoughts. Now, one person speaks at a time or I will make you sit in silence. I am your captain, you listen to me. Understood?" Sydney's hand shot up. "What, Sydney?"

"Well, um, if you would, please don't say the words 'sit in silence', because you're giving me flashbacks of when I went to that annoying boarding school and one person would talk out of turn then our mean teacher would force everyone to sit in silence, which I think is unfair, but then I tried to get revenge on that girl and I got..."

"Sydney, is this irrelevant?" I asked.

"Yes ma'am," she nodded.

"Alright, we have things to do. Sawyer will speak... and please let him speak... and then we will go on from there. You will be silent if someone else is speaking. I know you hate this, but you guys have got to get it together. No more fighting over clearing your throat and whether or not you're a chicken." I had finally gotten them all to be quiet. I was sure Sawyer really didn't have anything important to say, but I let him speak.

"What I was trying to say," he started, "is that it is not a good idea to go through that passage with bandits when we can just go around it."

He actually had a good point, but the passage was still the only way in. "Look," I reasoned, "any other way we could go is too rocky or has whirlpools or rapids. So, the only way is through the passage."

Ryker got up from his seat with an annoyed look on his face. That was, annoyed or *angry*.

"Belle, I've tried to tell you time after time. Bandits are dangerous! What are we to them? Five helpless kids. We can't fight them off! I think our lives are more important than your stupid parrot!" Ryker yelled angrily.

"Be quiet Ryker!" Sawyer stood up. "I don't care what you think, but I want Donna back just as much as Belle does. And I'm sure we would both give our lives just to make sure she's safe. If you can't live with that you can just leave, because we don't accept jerks like you!"

The whole situation sent my emotions into a confusing rage. I felt like I should hate him, but I didn't. I almost wanted to hate him, but I couldn't. I knew he was almost robbed or kidnapped when he joined the Stowaways, but that was over.

I knew I could do nothing to make myself stop having feelings for him, and I knew he wasn't a bad person. I knew that I made mistakes, too. But at the same time, I was furious at him. At the same time, I didn't care whether I felt anything for him or not. All of the thoughts I could ever think came to me all at once. No matter what, Ryker had taken it too far.

"Listen, Ryker!" I stormed, "Sawyer's right! I know you had a little *incident,* but you need to grow up. I have something to take care of and I can't let your fear hold me back. I admit that I'm not perfect, but Donna is not stupid and I know what I'm doing. So if you can't tolerate me as your captain, then you can leave the crew."

"You don't know what you're doing!" he shouted. " Just listen to me for once. I'm not trying to be rude, I'm just trying to protect you because you can't protect yourself!"

"Ryker, you can go now," I ordered.

"But you…"

"Now."

That night I stayed awake thinking. He had no right to treat me like that. I felt as though I should have just kicked him out right then and there. The real problem was I couldn't let him go. I could see the good in him. I knew that he really was a good person. He was only afraid for all of us. But then I remembered something. He specifically said "protect *you*." I remembered that the whole time he seemed to center everything around *me* and *my* safety.

"Why was he so specific?" I thought. "What don't I know?"

The Passage of Shadows

The next morning came. I got out of bed and opened my door only to find a pitiful and sorry-looking Ryker. He seemed so sad and pathetic.

"Belle," he started, "I am so stupid. I'm sorry about last night. I didn't mean it like that. I just didn't want you to get hurt. I know you can protect yourself. We need to go to that island. And I know I was too harsh at Shark Island. You didn't know that was the place. I've been a jerk lately. I'm sorry. I was just tired last night. That's all… really."

"I get it," I said. "You don't want to take any chances. And I should have known better. There was a lot on my mind and I was a little stressed about making everyone happy and going to Lost Island…" I hesitated. I almost gave away my secret. "And other things."

Something seemed strange about him. I knew he was sorry, but he wasn't just tired. No. There was something else. He had been hiding something. He did not speak to me as much, and when he did it was either just for crew meetings or he was trying too hard to win something from me. I just didn't know what it was he wanted. I thought maybe he wanted a promotion or something I owned. It was so strange especially for him because I knew that he was more mature than what he was displaying.

"Ryker," I asked. "Is something wrong?"

"No," he replied. "No, nothing's wrong."

"You've just been… different lately. You don't seem like yourself. I honestly don't think you were just tired last night."

"I'm fine, but you don't seem like you're just stressed," he said. "You usually are more sure of yourself. You seem distracted. You're not thinking about things and just going with what the others say so that you can please them. Tell me the *truth*. Is something actually wrong, or is it just me?"

"What do I do?" I thought. "Do I tell him that I have completely fallen in love with him and that he is the only thing I can think about? Do I tell him that I was overcome the moment I laid eyes on him? Do I lie and say that I am just stressed and it's nothing to worry about? No, I can't do that because I would never forgive myself. I…"

"Belle," Alice tugged at my sleeve. "Are we almost at Parrot Island? I miss Donna."

"I know you miss Donna, but we haven't even gone anywhere," I said.

"But Belle," Sawyer whined, "I want to fight the bandits, and I want to go to Lost Island, and I want my spy-glass back!"

Stop it, Sawyer," I scolded.

"Sawyer, I've seen you practice your sword fighting," Ryker added. "I'm not going to sugarcoat it. You're worse than Sydney."

"Ryker does have a point," I put in. "We'll go in a few minutes. Go do something useful."

Alice and Sawyer went on and did as they wished. Ryker and I hoisted the sails to set off. The wind was brisk and blowing south. It only took us a couple of hours to get to the passage.

"Everyone!" I called them. "Okay, we are about to sail into the passage leading to Parrot Island." Sawyer's face lit up with excitement. "And no, Sawyer. You still stink at sword fighting. Now, here's the plan. We are going to put the map in a chest in my room so that no one can get to it.

"Sydney, you need to stay in my room with the door locked and guard the chest. You also need to be there for first aid if anyone gets injured. Ryker is going the steer the *Pegasus* through the passage while I watch for any bandits. We don't want to run into them, and yes, Sawyer, I know you want to. Sawyer and Alice, you're staying with Sydney. Sorry."

Sawyer's eyes widened in shock. He was furious. "You're not sorry! You don't think I can fight. Well, guess what. I don't care! I will fight! Mutiny! Mutiny!" Sawyer drew his sword and began to slash it about in every direction. He was having a terrible fit and did not seem to know a thing about what he was doing. I knew he didn't actually want to start a mutiny, so I picked him up, set him down on my hammock, and locked the door to my room.

Everyone else got where they needed to be and we pulled into the passage. It was foggy and gloomy and it was difficult to see anything. I wondered if we should even be going through the passage. It seemed so unpredictable and mysterious.

It was easy to tell that there was danger lurking somewhere. I wanted to turn back, and I was almost going to approach Ryker and tell him to stop the ship, but as I looked at him something prevented me. He looked so confident and undisturbed. He didn't have to worry about whether or not to go in, he just did as he was told and respected my decision. He knew we had to get Donna back, even though he and Donna never really got along. I knew it, too.

The *Pegasus* crept through the passage. Everyone was silent. Not a sound was made except for the creaking of the ship moving in the channel. There was no wind, only a mist rising up from the water. Tall jagged rocks towered over us. The path was narrow. Even the slightest creak or rock made an echo back and forth, never ceasing.

I watched and listened intently, fearing who or what could come out of that eerie mist. Suddenly, I began to hear footsteps, and then voices. I tried to find out where the sounds were coming from, but I couldn't make them out due to the resounding echoes of the passage.

I walked over to Ryker and whispered, "Stop the ship. Drop the anchor slowly… and quietly."

He nodded and did as I told him. I looked about the passage, and I could almost catch the image of four black boots quietly walking along the cliff. Then, they disappeared behind the fog.

Just then, a rock shot out of the mist a shattered as it hit the other wall of the passage. Rattled, I whirled around and then heard a splash in the water behind me. I turned again, confused and alarmed. A hand gripped my shoulder and covered my mouth. Before I could think to fight back an ugly and dirty man had pinned me to the wall of the cabin. A second one grabbed my wrists and tied them. I was so shocked that I couldn't even move!

The first bandit was lanky, with a long chin, a short and scratchy-looking beard, and a bony face. He had about five missing teeth and two gold ones. His hands were bony and his fingernails were dirty. He had a bandana tied around his head. As I looked at him more closely I realized that he looked pretty easy to take over. The second had a tonsure haircut with a shaggy beard and two nose rings. His teeth were either rotten or metal. He had a scar on both cheeks.

As I looked at the two of them I saw that Ryker had seen what had happened. He picked up his sword and began to slowly sneak up behind the first bandit. Then, he stopped, turned around, and got my sword. He continued toward the bandits.

"Don't look so confused," the first said. "Looky here, me and my good pal, Jonathan, crept up to the top of that cliff, threw that rock, you turned, jumped in the water, you turned, swam under the ship, climbed onto the deck, and now we're here."

I was surprised to see that the bandits were not total numbskulls. But that didn't last long. Ryker was behind the first bandit. He took long enough to get there. The bandit was clueless. Ryker swung his sword in front of the bandit and held it just below his neck.

"Jack!" Jonathan exclaimed. He kept a tight grip on my wrists. "Jack, don't move. Eh, you! Yeah, I'm talking to you. Let the poor man go! Yeah, you let him go, or I'll...I'll... I'll take that... uh... that barrel... and... uh... run away with it!"

"What kind of a threat is that?" Ryker asked. "Sure, take the barrel. Then, I'll be through with both of you."

"Please!" Jonathan begged. "Let the poor chap go."

"I'll let your friend go if you let her go," Ryker said. "Deal?"

"Fine," Jonathan went to untie the cord around my wrists. "Nope. Never mind. I can't untie this knot. I made it too tight, and now it is permanent. Well, sorry, lad."

"Cut it with your sword." Ryker moved his own sword closer to Jack's throat.

"Cut it with your sword, Jonathan!" Jack yelled. Then, all of the color drained from his face. "We left our swords on the ship."

"Wow, you two are stupid. Here," Ryker gave Jonathan my sword with his other hand. I thought Ryker had lost his mind until I remembered that he knew that Jonathan would never think to start a fight. Jonathan cut the cord and Ryker let Jack go.

"Give me that!" I went to take my sword back, but Jonathan wouldn't let go of the handle and the blade was too sharp to grab.

"Feisty little girl! Watch this!" He threw the sword into the water.

"Thanks a lot, Ryker," I said and rolled my eyes.

"As if you knew he would think to do that!" Ryker replied.

"Hey, Jonathan, we know this lad. Ryker, is it? Remember, Jonathan, he's that kid we tried to rob, but then he got on a big boat and disappeared."

"I knew that!" Jonathan lied. "That was this boat, dummy!"

Fear filled Ryker's eyes. He suddenly realized who these men were, and evidently, they were the same dangerous men who were chasing him down the beach when we met him. I could tell by the terror on his face why he dreaded coming here.

Jack grabbed Ryker. "Long time, no see, eh? 'You still got that old wallet of yours?"

"Yeah, Ryker. Give us that fine wallet. And while you're at it, give us the girl!" Jonathan walked closer to Ryker.

"Get off of this ship. I am the one with the sword, and I'm not afraid to use it," Ryker stammered.

"Yes, you are." Jonathan grabbed Ryker's neck and threw his sword into the water, too.

"Oh, no!" I thought. "That dummy is gonna kill him! Belle, stop thinking like that, or you will sound like a dummy, too. Hey, wait a minute. We have an advantage. Jonathan was dumb enough to take our swords and throw them out instead of using them for their own benefit. We're saved!"

I pulled Jonathan's beard until he was screaming and had to let go of Ryker. "Stop!" I shouted. "Before you kill him, you may want to reconsider. Only he knows where his wallet is. So, if you really want the wallet, you'll have to let him go so he can tell you."

Ryker gave me a look, probably saying that he had no idea where his wallet was and no intention of giving it away. I winked at him to let him know it was a trick. His face turned bright red. I assumed it was because he couldn't breathe. Jonathan let him go and Ryker said, "Yes… yes, it's in that… that… barrel, over there."

Jack hopped over to the barrel and stuck his head inside. "Jonathan, we've been tricked, There ain't nothin' in here but some measly spy-glass." He pulled it out and looked through it.

"Oh, well. It's useless. I can't see a thing. So sad to put all that pure gold to waste." He threw it into the water just like any other useful thing they had stolen from us.

Jonathan grabbed me and tied me to the mast. I had no sword. I could only kick and scream and hope Ryker would fight. Jonathan slapped Ryker across the face.

"Listen, boy!" he yelled. "You're weak! You always have been. You think you've grown up since the last time we saw you, but you haven't. You are nothing! I say you are and your father would have, too. Don't you get it? That's why he was planning to send you into the army… to get rid of you because you're just good-for-nothing trash. You're a coward. And I bet you're too scared to tell Little Missy this." Jonathan whispered into Ryker's ear something I couldn't make out. Even before he whispered it Ryker looked overcome and beaten. But now his face was filled with shock and horror.

I hated seeing him like that, so heartbroken, so powerless. Ryker did not even try to fight back as Jack took him and tied him to the other mast.

Now the only thing left to hope for was a miracle. And we got one. Sawyer broke down the door to my bedroom and he, Sydney, and Alice all came running out armed only with combs.

It did not take long for Jack to fling Sawyer into the mist and for Sydney to come running after him. Our only hope left was Alice, a four-foot-tall and weaponless seven-year-old.

"Awww. Isn't she cute!" Jack exclaimed. "Now, be a good little girl and go back into your room."

Alice walked up to him and smiled. She looked sweet and innocent... too innocent to fight. I was wrong, because right then and there she swung her fist forward and punched him right in the stomach. Jack flew backward and cried in pain.

"Jack, don't be such a baby. She's just an average little girl. Hey, where'd she go?" Jonathan exclaimed. Alice ran behind him and jumped onto his back. She hung onto his neck with one arm and pulled out her comb. I could see where this was going. She took it and pulled it through Jonathan's matted beard. He screamed and flung her off of his back. Alice only giggled. She got up and began to hop up and down on top of Jack. Jonathan picked her up by her collar.

"Looky, here, young lady," he said. "Don't you cause any more problems, or I'll tie you up like I did to your buddy, Ryker."

"Okay!" Alice exclaimed as she swung her legs forward into Jonathan's stomach. She wrapped them around his belly and held up her comb and grinned. This time she combed down from his tonsure to his eyes straight down his beard. He let go and pushed her away. As both bandits reached for her, she grabbed their heads and smashed them together.

"Retreat!" Jack screamed as the two of them ran to the edge of the ship.

"She's a demon!" Jonathan shouted. "Here to steal our very souls!"

They ran away and into the fog crying like little girls.

Sydney jumped onto the deck with Sawyer. "Ha!" she cheered. "Bet you didn't know we'd come back with swords, now did you? Prepare to... oh. They're gone. Um... hi. Are these you guys' swords? Also, where did the bandits go?" Sydney looked confused and embarrassed.

"Alice fought them off!" I giggled.

"You mean I missed all of the fighting? Darn," Sawyer pouted.

"I'm not surprised," Sydney said. "That black eye I had a month ago, that was Alice. So, how'd you do it?"

"Wait," I said. "Before we go into a big long story can you two free us?"

Sydney and Sawyer released me and Ryker. We ate dinner and chatted and laughed over Alice's victory, but the whole time Ryker never said a word. I didn't know that what Jonathan said would mean so much to him. I guess I would be the same if I was told that I was unwanted and good for nothing. I tried to talk to him, but I couldn't get anything out of him. I had no choice but to stop even trying to make things better. I had to focus on Donna, now.

Love Birds

The next day came. We kept on going through the passage. There were no signs of any bandits and I was able to relax a little. The further we went the less tense we became. The fog cleared and light came through.

I realized that the passage had no name. It needed a name. I assumed it was too unknown and too unpopular for it to have a name, but it was not unknown to me. It was mysterious, cold, dark, and dangerous. It was like it was made up of a million shadows that could jump out at you any second. I suddenly came up with the perfect name. I picked up the map and an ink pen and wrote next to the passage, "The Passage of Shadows."

The *Pegasus* approached a bright and welcoming island. There were millions of parrots flying around and singing. We dropped the anchor and walked onto the island. A red and blue parrot stopped us and began to scream, "*Squawk! Squawk!* Intruders! Leave, or we shall peck at your heads for all eternity! Leave! Leave, or the wrath of the parrots shall haunt you! *Squawk! Squawk!*" He spread out his wings and squawked as loud as he possibly could.

"Excuse me, but why do you think we're intruders? We mean no harm," Alice said.

A turquoise parrot flew down and said, "Pirates come here and kidnap parrots to make them into slaves."

"Oh, no! We don't mean any trouble," I said, "You see, our parrot, Donna, belongs with us and we think she's here. She loves us and we really miss her."

A fat purple parrot with a French accent peeked out of a tree and said, "She probably ran away because she did not want to be your slave."

"She's not our slave. She is our friend," Sydney argued, "Could you please just tell us where she is?"

"We know nothing of this Donna," the turquoise one replied.

My heart sank. Donna wasn't here. I should have known. Ryker was right. We had come all this way for nothing. Going through the passage was for nothing. Donna had meant everything to me and now she was gone forever. If she wasn't here, she could be anywhere in the world. Even a parrot could be a best friend, and that's exactly what Donna was to me. Everything seemed worthless knowing she was gone.

"You know her," Ryker prompted. "Green, with one purple feather, one blue, and one aqua. We lost her about a week ago."

"Oh, Princesse's wife-to-be!" the red one exclaimed. "I see, you came for the wedding. There will be flowers and cake, and I am the priest. It's in two days."

"Wait a minute!" Sawyer argued. "Birds can't throw weddings, and Donna never told us she was getting married, and to who? Some guy named Princesse! That sounds like 'princess', and princesses are girls."

"Alas! A sad story, it is. You see, Princesse's owner thought he was a girl, so she named him Princesse, French for 'princess'. So, he has had a lady's name ever since," the red parrot bowed his head shamefully.

I could not believe what was happening. First, Ryker had paid attention to the three different colors of Donna's head feathers? First, Donna was actually here? And second, she was getting married to someone with the name 'princess.'

"Where is she?" I asked.

"The center of the island," the purple parrot said. "Follow me."

The purple parrot led us through the island and to a tree filled with white blossoms and candles.

"We have already taken it upon ourselves to decorate their home for the wedding. We are anxiously awaiting the day! I will go in and get them." He flew into the tree.

"Ryker!" Donna swooped out of the tree and stumbled into Ryker's startled face. "Oh, Ryker, how I've missed you! I have missed your angry expressions when I annoy you! Oh, Ryker, you are the only Stowaway I missed! *Squawk! Squawk!* I could kiss you!" Donna began to peck at Ryker's face as though she were actually kissing him.

"Donna, why are you marrying a princess?" Sawyer asked.

"His name is Princesse, and he's very handsome. And you should really be more polite about my fiance," Donna replied.

"Get off of my face!" Ryker complained.

"Donna," I said, "we need to talk. What's going on? Why did you run away?"

"I said get off of my face!" Ryker pushed Donna away and dusted himself off.

"Boredom," Donna answered. "I was tired of doing the same thing all of the time. So, I came here and fell in love. *Squawk!* Princesse! Come meet my friends!"

Princesse flew down beside Donna and chirped, "*Bonjour! Bonjour!* You must be Donna's pirate friends. I am Princesse."

"Nice to meet you, Princesse," I said. "I am Belle Smith, the captain…"

"I do not talk to girls who wear pants. A disgraceful thing!" Princesse exclaimed.

"Belle can wear whatever she wants to! Be nice to her!" Donna argued.

"Look, Princesse. Donna belongs with us, whether you like it or not. So, you can come with us or you two love birds will just have to split up. We are not leaving without her," Ryker said. I was surprised at how hard he was trying to get Donna back. I had no idea why he wanted her back so badly, but he had been submissive to the idea ever since we entered the passage. Was it for Donna, himself, or the crew?

"You are no man to boss me around! Donna will marry me! And who are you, anyway? The girl with pants' boyfriend? *Squawk! Squawk!*" Princesse screamed.

Sydney clapped her hand over her mouth, but Sawyer began to open his. Did Sawyer know my secret?

"Shut up! Don't talk! Say nothing!" Ryker shouted as he dived on top of Sawyer then ran behind a tree. I tried to stand there without looking suspicious, but that was very hard to do considering the fact that my face was as red as red could possibly be. But Ryker seemed to be acting even weirder than I was. Alice grinned from ear to ear. What did she know?

"No! No! There is absolutely nothing going on between the two of us. That is very unlikely. Impossible, even! I have no feelings for him whatsoever," I lied as I crossed my fingers behind my back. I whispered to Sydney, "Not a word, Sydney. Just keep that little mouth of yours shut until we leave, okay?"

She whispered back, "My mouth is big, not little. That's why I had to cover it before anything slipped out. But yes, I will say nothing of the sort."

"Are you sure?" Princesse asked Ryker. "Because you look suspicious and she looks suspicious."

"Yes, he's sure," Sawyer said. "It's not Ryker who likes Belle. I, in fact, am madly in love with her. Ryker is in love with Sydney, and Alice is in love with me."

"No, I'm not! You're not even cute! And you're too old for me!" Alice stepped on Sawyer's foot.

"Fine. The whole thing was a lie. Belle's the one that likes me," Sawyer lied.

"Oh, be quiet, Sawyer," I said. "You know I don't like you. As Alice said, you're not even cute."

"Wait. What did I miss? Who's in love with who?" Donna asked.

"No one! Can we please move on from the love interests?" I was getting very annoyed. This was the most uncomfortable subject possible.

"No! I am the boss and if I want to talk about love interests, then we will talk about love interests! Now, let me talk about my abundant love for my beautiful bird, Donna."

"*Ooh, la, la!*" Donna exclaimed. The two parrots cuddled close and chirped together.

"Yuck! Love birds!" Sawyer covered his eyes and turned around.

"You're not the boss, Princesse!" Sydney exclaimed. "And we are not talking about love interests! Now, can we please talk to Donna?"
"*Squawk!* Anything you say Princesse can hear, too!" Donna said.

"Fine," I said. "Donna, do you remember about two weeks ago when we said we were going to Lost Island?"

"Nope," Donna stuck her beak in the air.

"She flew below deck calling you 'mean Captain.' Remember?" Alice recalled.

"Well, while you were sulking or pouting or whatever you were doing, we decided that we would go to Lost Island to find its treasure. It's the most dangerous place in the world. We think we can do it, but, Donna, what's the point if you're not there? Please, Donna. We've missed you. We can even stay for the wedding and Princesse can come with us," I said.

"*Squawk! Squawk!* Good Captain! Count me in!"

We jumped around, our hearts filled with joy until Princesse chimed in, "No! I will have nothing of the sort! Donna stays!"

"But, Princesse, we can go together. It will be fun!" Donna argued.

"No!" Princesse squawked, "You stay here and do as I say just like any common housewife!"

"Common!" Donna squealed. "I am no common parrot! Do you have no respect for me?"

"You are my property!"

"No, I'm not! I thought you loved me! In two days we vow to love each other forever!"

"Be quiet! You are mine and you have no right to talk to me that way! *Squawk! Squawk! Squawk!*" Princesse spread out his wings in a rage.

"I am not yours until the wedding! And I will never be yours because the wedding is called off! Goodbye, Princesse!"

As Donna went to lead us out I realized that Ryker was gone! When we finally found him, he was sitting alone. He looked miserable. For a split second, I thought he was crying, but I knew better than that. I had never seen Ryker cry, since the day I had met him. Something was seriously wrong. Something had seemed off about him for a while now, but this was the most uncanny of all.

I told him to get up and follow me to meet the rest of the crew. The six of us walked (or flew) to the shore and boarded the *Pegasus*.

We once again crept through the Passage of Shadows, following the same routine as the last time. But this time, feeling less afraid to break the silence, I walked over to Ryker and began to speak. I had to know what was troubling him so terribly right away.

"Alright, you're busted. What's up?" I asked.

"Nothing. I just need my space," he replied.

"No," I said. "No. You're lying. You haven't been yourself for a long time. And then what happened today? What is your deal? I'm not trying to be nosey. Just tell me the truth!"

"And *you're* lying," he said, "so, maybe you're the one who's busted. Maybe you should just tell *me* the truth."

"I admit that I have been bothered lately, but it's not something that I would talk about to most people," I argued.

"So you don't have to tell me, but I have to tell you?" Ryker raised his voice.

"I don't want you to torture yourself!" I shouted.

"I can't tell you or anyone!" he yelled.

"Does it have anything to do with Jack and Jonathan?" I asked. Even if I had to play a guessing game, I would get it out of him.

"Yes."

"Is it part of what Jonathan said to you?"

"Yes," Ryker admitted.

"That's it!" I exclaimed. "It's whatever Jonathan whispered, isn't it?"

"Belle, just leave me alone."

"No! What did he say?"

"I can't tell you! I can't tell anyone! Leave me alone!" Ryker thundered.

"I don't care, you're telling me now!" I ordered.

"Fine," Ryker said. "Jack and Jonathan were sent to get you. Your old crew is after you. They want you back. I don't know why, but they do. I'm sorry. I should have told you before now. I just… I just couldn't. We need to be watching. We might need to turn back. The *Cobra* may even be in this passage."

No More Secrets

I stared at Ryker in shock. I could hardly fathom what he had just said. What did they want with me? I was nothing to them. I just stood there in a trance. Everything came back. I remembered being called 'worthless' and 'stupid'. I remembered being whipped every day by the captain. Captain Clark was the most evil person I had ever laid eyes on.

The worst thing about him was the snake that he kept in a cage below deck. The captain sent in a crew member every day to beat it and make it hate people, but he treated it as though it were his prized possession. So, when they were losing a fight, they would unleash their cobra. It would attack anyone the captain ordered it to. It was their most feared weapon.

"How did this happen? How did they know where we would be?" I was still baffled.

"I don't know, but the path is too narrow to turn back," Ryker said, his voice low and serious.

"We can't fight them," I said with tears running down my face. "We'll give them what they want. I don't care what it is."

"They want you," Ryker said.

"Then I'll go with them. It's the only way."

"No," Ryker protested. "You can't just turn yourself over to them. We can leave the *Pegasus* behind and go back."

"The water's too deep for Alice and Sawyer to swim in," I said as I turned my eyes to the floor, "and we can't climb the rocks. We don't have any rowboats. There's no escape."

"You can't go with them!" Ryker declared. "We can't lose you!"

The truth was that I would never turn myself over to them. They were evil to me and treated me like a slave. I would have to fight, but I didn't want the Stowaways risking their lives for me. Only there was no more time to think. A massive cobra emerged from the mist. The ship it was carved into came behind it. It was too late. The wretched men of my childhood were already here. I stared into the eyes of Captain Clark. He was just as terrible as I had remembered.

I walked to the very front of the *Pegasus* and said, "And so we meet again. You know, I actually thought I would never see you again. Too good to be true, I guess."

"Shut up and get on the ship," Clark yelled.

"What do you want me for?" I drew out my sword.

"A little birdie told me you were a good fighter. I wondered if you might take your chances and go to Lost Island. So, I paid that salesman ten thousand pounds of gold to give me information about you. He told me about how the ship drifted away in the storm and that little green parrot flew off. See, he knew about Parrot Island and he knew you would try to get her back and he knew about that passage. So, we sent Jack and Jonathan to go get you, but they're too stupid to even remember to bring swords. So, the only way was for me to do the job myself. Oh, I'm sorry we underestimated you. We could really use you to rob King William up in London." The captain walked onto the *Pegasus*.

"I would die before I join you," I said.

"But you'll be no use to us if you're dead," the captain said with a sweet and insincere voice.

"Good," I replied as I backed up.

"So, you would die, but will they? You see, if you don't get on my ship right now, I will kill all your little friends and you'll have no reason to stay here, *Captain*." He drew closer and closer.

"Never!" I swung my sword across Clark's arm. The startled captain swung his own just over my head as I ducked below it. I had fought many battles, but the worst of all had just begun.

Our swords clashed and banged against each other. One of my arms and one leg had blood streaming down but I would fight no matter what. I would never turn myself over to them. Except for one thing, though. I didn't want Ryker to fight.

He had only even learned to do hand-to-hand combat a year ago. He was good, but I would never place any bets on him. He wouldn't last a moment with Clark.

I was barely hanging on when I saw my chance. Clark was holding his sword close to the ground with a loose grip. I kicked it out of his hand and it glided to the other side of the ship. I ran to pick it up in pain as my foot bled where it had knocked out his sword. With the two swords, I backed him up to the golden railing and crossed them in front of his neck.

I thought he would surrender, but he put his big hands on the blades and bent them. He snatched them from my grip, threw them down, took out his whip, and whipped me across the face. I was in such pain that I couldn't move. He grabbed my braid and clutched my face.

"Listen, Little Missy," he shouted. "You are nothing compared to me. You thought you could get away, did you not? Well, guess what. You can't! No matter how hard you try, I will always hunt you down and take you with me. You are mine and…"

"Get away from her!" Ryker flung his sword across the captain's wrist and chopped his hand clean off! Why was he being so foolish? He was not ready for this!

"Well, tough competition, I guess," the captain mocked. "Come on, guys!" About twenty pirates leaped onto the *Pegasus*. We were outnumbered, greatly. Only this time, I couldn't lose hope no matter how painful the battle would be. If I were to die, I would die fighting.

I didn't think things could get any worse when I heard my bedroom door burst open. Sydney, Sawyer, Donna, and Alice all ran out. Alice was only seven and Sawyer wasn't much older! They'd be dead in seconds!

I ran over to Sydney and said, "What on earth do you think you're doing? You'll be killed, much less Sawyer and Alice."

"Belle, I'm fourteen," Sydney argued. "The Stowaways can do more than you think. Just trust us."

"Okay," I said," I trust you, but if you hear the word 'cobra', I want you to run. Grab the rest of the crew and run to the safest place you can think of. If they resist, be forceful."

"What do you mean? What cobra?" Sydney demanded.

"Don't ask," I said. I began to fight, looking back at the rest of the crew. I soon realized the fact that I could put my trust in them. I could count on them. It wasn't foolish of Ryker to fight. I wouldn't have lasted much longer if it weren't for him. Just because I was the captain didn't mean I was on my own. But if the cobra came out, they wouldn't last. I knew things they didn't know.

I was fighting two men at once, who were both about to faint. One had an eye patch. When he looked away, I threw my sword into his face and his other eye became useless. He thought that he could fight blind, so he slashed his sword into the other pirate's arm, thinking he was me. The two began to fight each other and I ran to help Alice.

She was also fighting two pirates. They were still in good shape, but they had no swords. Alice was actually better off without one. She was aggressive, but I had only ever learned to fight with a sword. So, I let her be because she was fine.

Night came and we had been fighting for an hour. I was fighting hand-to-hand with a big man, probably six feet tall. I was drenched in blood and in pain. I tried not to pass out, but every second I felt like I would, more and more. I kept fighting. I knew that if the cobra stayed in its cage and if I kept going, we could beat them. The pirate was almost down when I heard a loud cry. Ryker!

I ran to the front of the *Pegasus*. Ryker was fighting the captain. The entire side of his face had been cut. That was the only damage so far. He had only been fighting the captain for a few minutes, but he wouldn't last much longer. I pushed him away and began to take his place in the fight. Clark had become angrier and was more aggressive now. But I was, too. We fought and fought, both cut and bruised.

I soon realized I had a good opportunity. I ducked and swung my sword across his leg. Captain Clark fell to the ground. I ran to the back of the ship. I had to stop for at least a few seconds. I was leaning against the cabin, struggling to breathe. It wasn't long before I heard the most dreadful words I could hear.

"Send out the cobra!" the captain exclaimed, with fury in his eyes. "Those five. Save Blondie."

Sydney grabbed Sawyer and Alice and threw them into my room. I ran to get Ryker, but he resisted.

"Belle, I'm not going to leave you!" he screamed.

"I know things you don't," I shouted as I pinned him to the rail. "You can't fight the cobra. Now, go hide with the others!"

"No! Why don't you trust me?" Ryker yelled.

"Why can't you just get to safety?" I pleaded, almost starting to cry. I couldn't lose him.

"Because," Ryker said, "I love you. You can call me crazy all you want. I've loved you since the moment I saw you. I admire everything about you. I just don't want to take any chances. I'd give my life for you, I really would. Just let me help."

"I love you, too. You're everything to me. But this is my battle to fight. I'm sorry," I said just before I pushed him over the rail. He fell into the water as I began to sob. I knew he would find a place to get out. Ryker was better off in the water than fighting the cobra.

The captain and his crew boarded their ship to spectate as an eight-foot-long cobra slithered onto the *Pegasus*. I didn't know how I would fight it. It tried to slide under my door. I threw my sword down on it, but it did not do much damage.

The snake only became angry... angry at me. It raised its head and hissed. It charged at me, trying to bite me. I was barely able to dodge its huge fangs. I kept trying to fight the crawling beast, failing to hurt it and only making it angrier. I also became angrier.

I finally was so infuriated, so in pain, so hurt by the dreadful memories, that I stepped on its head, picked up its tail, and chopped it in half. It was dead. I threw it into the water.

"Retreat!" the captain screamed. All of the men, dumbfounded and baffled, staggered into their places. The *Cobra* backed into the mist as Clark shouted back to me, "I'll be back, and you're coming with me next time!"

I watched as the ship disappeared. Ryker swam through the water and climbed onto the *Pegasus*. The rest of the crew walked out of my room and began to cheer happily. I looked at Ryker. He seemed different now. He was braver and more sure of himself. I then realized that he had tried so hard to get Donna because he had cared. I smiled.

"We knew everything," Sydney said.

"Knew what?" Ryker asked suspiciously.

"You are mentally ill," Sawyer said.

"You told Sydney I was in love with Belle?" Ryker was dumbfounded. "I knew you were acting weird, you little brat! You betrayed me. Not only that, but you let me torture myself to win her approval? You..."

"Excuse me," Sawyer interrupted, "but I did not tell Sydney anything. It was Alice. She was spying. And we tried to tell you, but then Belle asked where Donna was and then everyone was busy. Don't blame me, blame Alice."

"You are such a traitor!" Alice smacked Sawyer in the face.

"I'm gonna sit down," I said. I was exhausted and throbbing in pain. I sat against the rail of the ship and sighed. Ryker left the conversation and sat down next to me.

"I had no idea," he said.

"I should have known," I said. "You're a terrible liar."

"You, too."

"No more secrets?" I held out my hand.

"No more secrets."

We shook hands and looked at each other awkwardly and giggled. But that nice feeling didn't last long. My head felt hot and my whole body was aching. I put my hands in my face and tried not to faint.

"You okay?" Ryker asked suddenly.

"No," I stammered. "I think I'm about to pass out. Go get Sydney. Hurry."

"Okay. You stay right there. I'll be back," Ryker stood up and ran to get Sydney, but before anything could be done, the world had become vague, black, and silent.

Biscuits

I opened my eyes and blinked. I was in Sydney's room. I was confused for a second because the last thing I remembered was Ryker going to get Sydney. Then I realized I had passed out. I still was surprised by the events of the night before. I couldn't believe I had fought my own captain... and won. I had defeated the cobra, and the Stowaways had sent the Sea Raiders running.

There was one thing I was still baffled at. Ryker had told me he loved me. It was so obvious looking back, but everything was chaos at the time. I was so stressed that I was oblivious to something right in front of me. I was glad I now knew.

"Belle! You're alive!" Sydney jumped up from the seat she was in. "You've been unconscious for an hour, which is way too long. We were all worried sick."

"I still can't believe what Ryker said to me…" I sat up, but Sydney pushed my head onto the pillow.

"Lay down," she ordered.

"You hurt me," I complained as I rubbed the bruise on the back of my head.

"Sorry, but you still should lay down. How are you feeling?"

"My head hurts from you banging it on the floor."

"Other than that."

"Fine," I replied.

"Good." Sydney pulled out a needle and thread.

My eyes widened. "Sydney, if I was unconscious for an hour, then why are you giving me stitches now? You know that makes me uncomfortable!"

"Belle, how dumb do you think I am?" Sydney asked. "This is for your pants."

"Oh," I cautiously sat up. One bruise was enough. Sydney began to start sewing.

"Tell me if I poke you," she said. "I know pain causes people to pass out, but I think it was also plainly from exhaustion. You've been working a lot lately, and you've also been stressed. Are you like me? Do you stay up till midnight thinking?"

"Is this going to be like one of Sawyer's therapy lessons?" I asked.

"Of course not," Sydney replied.

"Okay. Well, last night I was thinking about Ryker and going to find Donna. The night before we were looking for Donna, and the night before we also just had that conversation about Ryker. You know, maybe it would have helped if you had told me."

"About Ryker? Believe me, we were going to tell you, but then we found out Donna was missing. But I personally think the telling was up to him."

"I guess so," I said.

"I think you've been so stressed because you're trying to please everyone and do everything on your own. Is that right?"

"I don't want to be asking for too much. Aren't my problems for me to deal with?"

"Just because you're the captain doesn't mean you're alone. I can assure you, if I pull out a dictionary and look up the word 'captain', the word 'alone' won't be in the definition. We're your crew, which means your problems are our problems."

Sydney cut the end of the thread she was using. "Good as new, but your boots are a lost cause. I bet I have some old ones you can use, but I say just walk around barefoot until I find them."

I thanked her and gave her a hug. I went to bed, but this time I was able to sleep because I wasn't so troubled. What seemed the worst had passed. Lost Island was next.

The next day went by quickly. Sydney found her old boots and gave them to me. I rescued Ryker from Sawyer's therapy lesson. Then, he told me about a few days ago when Sawyer told him he was mentally ill. I was surprised to hear he believed it. It was a good day, with no crazy dangerous situations. Night fell and we were finally able to relax and have supper.

"Biscuits tonight. All of the plates are dirty, so just eat from the platter. You two share with the rest."

Sydney stared at Ryker and Sawyer. "Especially you, Ryker. And don't take a bite out of one and put it back on the platter, Sawyer. That's gross."

"I'll share these," Ryker said. "In fact, I'll share all of them. I won't take any for myself."

"That's nice," Sydney observed. "It's an insult, isn't it? Oh, don't be shy, Ryker. Tell me, what is wrong with my biscuits?"

"You really don't know?" Ryker asked.

"No, I don't," Sydney scoffed. "Because there's nothing wrong with them."

"Yes, there is. You really don't see it? There's no gravy," Ryker pointed out.

"Sydney! This is blasphemy!" Sawyer deliberately took a bite out of a biscuit and put it back.

"Sawyer, you... ugh!" Sydney was making it obvious how irritated she was. "Look, gravy is dangerous."

"What's so dangerous about it, Sydney?" I asked with a sly grin. I wanted to see how angry we could make her. I also wanted gravy.

"Oh, where can I begin?" she started. "It can burn you, it goes bad, people use it in catapults for mutiny, and you can drown in it."

"Those all seem very unlikely. Please explain." Ryker was satisfied by the aggravated look on Sydney's face.

"Alice was burnt by gravy that was too hot one time, it does go bad, Alice and Sawyer made a gravy catapult that night you were at Seaside Scalawags, and... and... and I don't care about that last one!" Sydney finished with a scream.

"You're afraid of gravy?" Alice asked.

"No! Yes! I don't care anymore!" Sydney shrieked.

"But Sydney, you're always forcing everyone to unwillingly be logical, so I will force you," Sawyer said. "Ryker was afraid of those bandits, but he still went through that passage. So, shouldn't you go get me some gravy?"

"I'm not afraid of gravy!" Sydney yelled.

"So you'll go get it?" he asked.

"If it'll get you to shut up!" Sydney stomped off into the kitchen and brought the gravy. She sat down next to Alice. I was on the other side of Alice, Ryker was across from me, and Sawyer was next to Ryker. It was not long before Sydney was upset again.

"I can't take it anymore!" she fumed. "Alice, we are switching seats right now!" Alice got up, looking confused, and they switched seats. Sydney and I both grabbed a biscuit, but she put hers down and sighed. "Belle, you, too?" She stood up with an annoyed look on her face. I switched seats with her.

"Sydney, are you mentally ill?" Sawyer asked. Ryker nudged him and gave him a look.

"I can't sit on the left side of left-handed people," she replied. "When I lift my arm, and they lift their arm, our elbows knock each other. And you know that when someone slightly touches me, it makes me anxious."

"I have seen many strange things in my life, but this is just dumb," Sawyer said. "Wait, wait, wait: who am I? Ooooh, I have anxiety issues. I'm afraid of gravy. I'm soooooo smart. Blah, blah, blah!"

"Sawyer, stop making fun of Sydney!" I interrupted.

"Yeah, don't make fun of her anxiety issues," Alice said. "Make fun of her liking that kid named Michael."

"Tell me everything!" Sawyer exclaimed.

"No!" Sydney shouted.

"So, when Sydney was at her boring school," Alice began, "she and some boy would stare at each other, like, every day. And so she was just in love. And…"

"*Boarding* school! *Boarding* school!" Sydney cried. "Not *boring* school! And you're telling the story all wrong! This is a very uncomfortable subject for me."

"Tell that to Princesse," I broke in.

"Go on," Sawyer urged.

"Well, um, maybe we shouldn't. I... I...um," Ryker stuttered.

"He's trying to say we shouldn't make fun of Sydney because he is in the same situation and he takes pity on her. He's just too prideful to actually say it," I clarified.

"Do people in love read each other's minds?" Sawyer inquired.

"I don't care about Ryker, but for Belle's sake, let's change the subject," Sydney agreed.

"Great," Ryker said. "Hey, Sydney, did you say when someone slightly touches you it gives you anxiety?"

"Yeah..." Sydney admitted.

"Okay," Ryker said. He smiled.

"Let me get this straight," I said. "When we were in the passage and I winked at you, your face turned red. Were you blushing or choking?"

"Oh, I was blushing. You didn't know that?" Ryker said.

"Belle, scoot over," Sydney grumbled.

"Let me guess; it gives you anxiety," Ryker said.

"Yes, I can't move," she complained.

"Great," Ryker said. I wondered why he especially seemed satisfied by Sydney being so annoyed. I peeked under the table. It was obvious why she was so upset. Ryker was kicking her.

"Ugh, who is kicking me?" Sydney grunted.

"No one." Ryker looked off into the distance, his face cunning and happy.

"Stop it, Ryker," Sydney whined.

"Why should I?" Ryker asked.

"Because I told you so." She stuck her nose in the air.

"I listen to Belle. I don't listen to you," Ryker said. Sydney rolled her eyes.

"It's because she's the captain," Sawyer said. "It's also because she's his wife."

"Wife? Wife?" I screeched. "I am not his wife!"

"Well, maybe not yet, but you will be, once Ryker proposes to you," Sawyer teased.

"Sawyer, you really make me cringe." Ryker informed him and scooted away.

"And you make me cringe. Stop kicking me!" Sydney broke in.

"No thanks." Ryker said.

"Stop!" she yelled.

"I don't have to," Ryker returned.

"Yes you do, because I said so!" Sydney screamed.

"You know, these biscuits are really good." Ryker took one bite and put it back.

"Ryker Collins, shame on you!" Sydney stomped over to the other side of the table.

"Belle Collins..." Sawyer muttered.

"I've had it with you! Stop kicking me, or you will suffer the consequences, Mister. Actually, no! You'll suffer the consequences now!" Sydney, in a hilarious rage, grabbed Ryker's hair and pushed him over the rail and into the water. I burst out in laughter. In fact, I was laughing so hard that I could hardly breathe.

"My work here is done!" Sydney announced and sat back down.

"Belle, w-why are you l-laughing?" Ryker climbed over the rail and fell into his seat. "I am c-cold, wet, and hungry, I inhaled s-salt water, and n-now my head hurts from where S-Sydney p-pulled my hair!"

"I'm sorry! I can't help it, it's funny!" I gasped, still laughing. "Do you need a blanket or something?"

"I'm freezing! Y-yes! I am about to d-die from fr-frostbite," he stammered, hardly able to talk because his lips had turned blue. I got up to get a blanket.

"You know, Ryker, Sydney probably wouldn't have pulled your hair if it weren't so long," Sawyer said. "I mean, you look like a girl."

"W-what? S-Sydney, d-do I look like a girl?" Ryker asked.

"No," she retorted. "You're too ugly."

I came back with the blanket and threw it over Ryker's head.

"Ryker, you look silly!" Alice giggled.

"S-silly is b-better than ugly," Ryker stuttered. "B-belle, do you think I'm ugly?"

"Why would she think you're ugly? She's in love with you," Sydney answered.

"Yeah, what she said," I replied, blushing.

"Hey, guys, I have unlocked the secret of magic!" Sawyer exclaimed. "Who will volunteer to have me pull a coin out of their ear? They get to keep the coin."

"Oh, me!" Sydney exclaimed. "I want money!"

"Step forth," Sawyer invited. Sydney got up and walked to Sawyer's chair. Sawyer stood up and held up a small coin.

"Now, for a coin to come out of her ear, there must first be a coin originally in her ear, correct? Great. Here we go!" Sawyer took the coin and shoved it into Sydney's ear!

"You know, maybe this is a bad idea," Sydney said uncomfortably. "I have plenty of money."

"Deeper!" Sawyer exclaimed and jammed the coin farther in. Sydney sounded as though she were choking for some reason. Sawyer removed his hand.

"Now to pull it out!" He went to pull it out, but did not. "That's odd. And *now* we shall pull it out. Oops. I think it's stuck."

"What!" Sydney shrieked and burst into tears.

"Let me see," I said. Somehow, the coin was stuck. I tried to help, but Sydney wouldn't stop moving.

"Don't hurt me!" she screamed.

"Hold still for a second," I said. "How did this happen?"

"I don't know," she confessed. "Once I had a tick in my eyelashes, and once my doctor had to pry my eyeglasses off my face. I've even lassoed a taste bud with my own hair, and I've eaten a rattlesnake. I've been through a lot, so don't hurt me!"

"Let me see. I bet I can pry it out." Alice jumped up.

"You'll scratch me!" Sydney squealed.

"Let me help!" Alice forcefully grabbed Sydney's head and dug her hand into her ear. Sydney was screaming and crying the whole time. Alice pulled the coin out and threw it at Sawyer. Everyone sat back down.

"I have another trick," Sawyer began.

"I am already against it," I stated.

"Great!" Sawyer exclaimed. "Close your eyes. I'm going to make these biscuits disappear."

"B-but I'm s-still hungry," Ryker said.

"Close your eyes!" Sawyer repeated. Before anything could be done, he had already thrown the biscuits behind him into the water.

"Well it looks like dinner's over," I said.

Everyone went to bed. It was very early and I was reflecting on the battle with Captain Clark. Then I remembered a face I had very briefly but distinctly seen. It was the face of Dylan Crow. I knew it well. I had hardly given the boy any thought in months.

I suddenly remembered how he had been there as long as I had remembered. He was two years older than me, and we shared the cargo hold in the *Cobra* to sleep in.

He was like an older brother to me. He was the one who had kept me alive all those years. He had been treated much worse than I had been. He stood up for me, but he was barely alive himself. I wondered what had become of him.   That brief glance brought everything back.

Preparing for the Journey

Two days passed. We expected to arrive at Lost Island in a day. We needed to start preparing, but I still was unsure whether or not I actually wanted to go. Everyone gathered on the deck to discuss our journey.

"Alright, everyone. We are about to have the adventure of a lifetime if we still want to go, you know," I said with an unsure voice. "I mean, people who go there fall into their own demise. So, I'm sure we won't be going."

"Wait, what? We're not going?" Alice asked, disappointed.

"Not going? Belle, why aren't we going?" Sydney joined in.

"You don't even want to," I advised.

"Yes, I do!" Sydney insisted. "Wait a minute. Are you just doing that thing where you act all insecure so you refuse to do something you really want to do?"

"I don't want to go there and then die," I said.

"Ryker, say something romantic," Sawyer begged.

"No," Ryker returned.

"Ryker, tell me more about your love life," Sydney begged. "Why did you fall in love with Belle? Is she pretty? Is she nice? Is she brave? Are you too chicken to answer?"

"She's the only one who doesn't irritate me," Ryker answered.

"I don't irritate you!" Alice tried to defend herself, knowing she was wrong.

"You pushed me over and stepped on me!" Ryker accused.

"*Squawk! Squawk!* I'm bored. I want a boyfriend. I want to go to Lost Island. I want cake. I want cake. I want cake," Donna whined.

"What's her problem? Donna, are you mentally ill?" Sawyer asked.

"Stop asking that," Ryker demanded. "Although, of course, she might be," Ryker bopped Donna on the head.

"I want cake. I want cake. I want cake. I want cake," Donna repeated," I want cake. I want cake. I want cake…"

"I think she's broken," Sydney giggled. "But seriously. Make her stop."

Ryker hit her on the head again and she stopped begging for cake.

"But really," Sydney stopped laughing, "Why aren't we going?"

"It's complicated," I said.

"Do you need therapy?" Sawyer asked.

"Look, Belle," Ryker said. "I know you want to go. You were so excited at first, but now you're refusing when you're not even scared to do it. You're just thinking too hard about it. You already know we're gonna succeed; you just deny it. Why?"

"If we die, I'll be responsible for it," I said.

"Yeah. I know. You've made that very clear. Answer the question," Ryker said.

"That's my answer," I mumbled.

"Too bad. Come up with a better one," Ryker replied.

"That's the only answer I can give you," I lied. Ryker looked into my eyes. He knew there was more. I tried not to look at him but my eyes kept diverting back and forth. It was almost as though Ryker was saying, "What about that agreement? I thought you said, 'No more secrets.' I already know enough. You may as well just say whatever else there is."

I suddenly burst into tears. "I want to go! I've wanted to ever since I was eight years old. It's my dream and... and I know we can do it I just... I just don't... I'm sorry. I'm not trying to ruin it for us all. I just can't take any chances on you guys. And I want to go. I really do, I just..."

"Okay, that's enough. Belle, you're a mess," Sydney interrupted and gave me her handkerchief. "Ryker, that is the second time this week you've made Belle cry by just looking at her. Also, I think your hair is weird. And yes, I enjoy insulting you."

"*Squawk! Squawk!* Don't worry, Belle. You're not a loser. But I will say it was a bad decision to marry that stupid boy," Donna started stroking my face with her wing.

"First of all, she did not marry me," Ryker said. "Second, I am not stupid. Third, my hair is not weird."

"*Squawk!* I know you didn't try to make Belle cry. She just has a lot of emotional issues," Donna screeched.

"Belle… Donna, stop rubbing her face… Belle, you are the bravest girl I have ever met. And I am absolutely positive that if you led us into our journey alive, then you'll lead us out alive."

"Awww! That's so sweet! You two are the cutest couple! Why did I not ship you two before?" Sydney exclaimed.

"Please, Belle?" Alice begged.

I really did want to go. Ryker had gotten through to me, and we did agree to not keep any more secrets. Also, I had already made up my mind to go. Ryker knew me. He knew I wanted to go and he believed in me. I wiped my tears away and smiled. "Okay, okay. We'll go."

Everyone rejoiced. We were really going to go to Lost Island. It was only a day away. I ran to get the map. I sat down to examine it and I noticed a note on the map that I had never seen before.

"Hey, look at this. There's something written on the map," I said.

"Read it! Read it!" Sawyer and Alice exclaimed.

"Alright," I said. I read the note aloud:

"I am a pirate with tons and tons of gold and jewels. I lost my family. I have no one to inherit my treasures. So, I have buried my treasure into the top of a mountain. It is on the deadliest island ever to be found by mankind. Surprisingly, you have gotten this far. You have the map. But be warned. The island is filled with poisonous animals and plants, geysers, quicksand, and traps. If you succeed, take the treasure. You deserve it. However, there is but

only one diamond- the one who finds it is my true heir. Although, chances are you won't succeed.

August twenty-third, fifteen hundred, twenty-five. Pedro Francisco"

"The man must have been Spanish or Portuguese," Sydney said," It makes sense because people from that area liked to explore. You know, like Prince Henry and the Conquistadors."

"The Conquistadors weren't Portuguese," Ryker commented.

"How would you know? You're stupid," Sydney retorted.

"Yeah, Ryker. You're stupid," Alice echoed.

"No, I'm not!" Ryker denied. "You don't actually think that, do you?"

"No," Sydney said, "but it's fun acting like we do."

"Okay, okay," I intervened. "No more joking about Ryker being stupid. Let's see. What do we need?"

"*Squawk!* Cake!" Donna exclaimed.

"No, we do not need cake. Can you even eat cake?" Ryker asked.

"Yeah! It's yummy!" Donna squawked.

"Who gave Donna cake?" I asked.

"Not me!" Alice shook her head with a sheepish grin on her red face.

"Alice, why'd you give Donna cake?" Sydney asked.

"She looked hungry!" Alice answered.

"Please don't start the thing you were doing while I was talking about Parrot Island!" I shouted.

"What?" Sydney asked.

"When we had to tie you up," Ryker answered.

"Now that was just mean," Sydney said. "Also, I'm not a dork and I'm not nerdy. You…"

"Did you not hear what I just said?" I interrupted. "Now, what do we need?"

"Food and water," Sydney said as she pulled out a checklist.

"Cake!" Donna contributed.

"No, Donna," I said. Donna should have never even tasted cake. Now, she would always want it.

"What kind of traps are there?" Sydney asked, "Do we need to solve riddles and do stuff like that? We may need paper, and a quill and ink, in case this guy decides to throw math problems at us."

"We need a rope," I said.

"A lantern," Ryker said.

"Oh! Oh! I know! Those matches you had in your pocket when you lit a fire in that shark's stomach!" Sawyer jumped up.

"It swallowed you?" Ryker exclaimed.

"No," I explained. "That was its mouth, not its stomach."

"Fine, it was the mouth," Sawyer said, "and it swallowed my sword. Then, it fell asleep. And then we punched out its teeth!"

"How do I not know any of this?" Ryker looked very confused.

"She never told because you shattered her heart with your own eyes," Alice retorted.

"That's dark," I said.

"You sound evil," Ryker observed. "Oh wait. You are evil. That is the only thing Sydney and I will ever agree on."

"Now, Ryker, I think there's a slight difference between evil and just causing a lot of physical pain," I said. "Isn't that right, Sydney?"

Sydney stared at the floor and gave no answer.

"Sydney?" I prompted.

"Oh, sorry," she said," I just thinking about the fact that we have a sofa on our deck."

"Haven't we had this sofa forever?" Alice asked.

"No," Sydney answered. "We got it right after we found Ryker. We were sailing one night when a big storm hit. There was also a trading ship nearby delivering things to the New World. Well, the storm turned into this mini-hurricane type-deal. So, we were barely surviving while Ryker hid in his room like a chicken. To sum it all up, the other ship ran into us, dropped some boxes, and we had a free sofa."

"I guess it isn't normal to have a sofa," I admitted, "but can we please get back to the list?"

"I think the only things left are our swords, first aid, and that's it," Sydney replied.
"Okay then," I said.

Everyone went back to doing whatever they were doing before. The *Pegasus* sailed toward Lost Island all day. That night, knowing we were almost there, I stayed up to see the approaching island. After only half an hour, I saw a tall mountain peak rise up against the moon. The silhouettes grew and multiplied. And then I saw it- Lost Island. The legendary place was so beautiful in the moonlight. The bottoms of the mountains were covered in lush plants. The mountains almost seemed to have a mist around them. The island looked as though it were keeping a secret. It had been completely hidden from the world besides me and other pirates who had taken the journey. It had a sensational power to it, a power that would be forced against us with all of its might. We were about to attempt the hardest thing we had ever done.

To Take the First Step

The long-awaited day had come. We were going to Lost Island. As the *Pegasus* became closer to the island, Sydney packed a bag with all of the things we would need. I finally dropped the anchor when the ship was in the rapids with the rocks jutting out of the water. The strange thing was that the rocks were moving with the water. Surely that wouldn't matter.

"Alright everyone, we are going to Lost Island!" I called for their attention. "Try to at least take some caution, Sawyer. Yes, you. And Sydney, I know the poison dart frogs might be cute, but for goodness sake, don't touch them! Alright. The rocks are moving, so getting to the island may be harder than it looks."

Everyone crowded at the rail. I climbed on top of it and jumped. I landed on a rock, but it abruptly sank. I fell off and was quickly pulled by the current. I was hitting my head on the rocks and could hardly move. The water was so strong I couldn't even come up for air. I struggled to at least get my hand above the surface. Just as I did, I felt someone grab me. Having a death grip, they pulled me up and my head submerged from the water to see Ryker. I climbed back into the ship, still panting for air.

"Hey, Ryker, what's that you were holding on to?" Sydney teased.

"Belle's hand... oh no," Ryker answered. "Why, Sydney? Why? I was trying to save her, and I didn't mean it like that and you know it."

"Did you enjoy it?" Sydney went on.

"No... yes," Ryker admitted.

"That thought never even came to my mind," I insisted. "I was just trying not to drown."

"What happened anyway?" Sydney asked.

"I don't know, but I think the legend was interpreted the wrong way," I said. "The rocks weren't standing in the water, they were floating. I landed too hard and it jerked me. It just doesn't make any sense."

"No, it doesn't," Ryker said. "Rocks don't float."

"Pumice does, and you'd know that if you didn't sleep half the time you were in school, you dingbat," Sydney said. "And pumice is a volcanic rock, which means one of those mountains is a volcano. It may even be an active volcano. We may even be standing on top of a mountain when it erupts. We could end up like the Pompeians. We…"

"That's dumb, Sydney," Ryker interrupted.

"It is completely possible. We have the worst luck in the world," Sydney argued.

"Surely our luck isn't that bad," I said.

"*Screech!* You two are annoying. Let me settle the argument. Sydney is overly superstitious. Ryker is a dingbat," Donna squawked.

"I am not a dingbat!" Ryker shouted.

"In Ryker's defense, Sydney does have a… vivid imagination," I said, trying not to be offensive. "But let's get to the point. It really shouldn't be that hard now. Just don't use too much force."

"And if you drown again, you can just hold hands with your only one true love. Has he kissed you yet? If he does tell me how that goes," Sawyer grinned.

"Alright, that's it!" Ryker growled and started whacking Sawyer on the head. "Stop... making... fun... of...my...love life!"

I rolled my eyes and climbed over the rail. This time, I lightly landed on another rock and caught my balance. I kept going toward the island in the opposite direction of the current. The others followed me close behind.

"*Squawk!* I can't jump. My legs are too short. We should turn back," Donna complained.

"But Donna," Alice reasoned. "You're a bird. You can fly. Did you not know that?"

"I knew that!" Donna squawked. "I was testing you. Of course, I know I can fly! I'm totally not lying right now. I totally..."

"You forgot you could fly?" Sawyer asked.

"*Squawk!* No!" Donna squealed

"Donna, why couldn't you have been something pleasant, something that doesn't talk?" Ryker asked.

"What are you saying? Do you dare to insult me? Shame on you!" Donna griped.

"Oh yeah, he called you stupid," Sydney recalled.

"And then Belle sent him below deck like a little baby," Alice added.

I stopped listening to them. I hated thinking about that night. I had wondered why he was so mean. I knew why he had snapped now. He wasn't trying to be rude. He had said, "protect *you*." He didn't want me to get hurt because he loved me. He didn't want me to feel as helpless as he had the day we met. He made a mistake, but he had his reasons behind it.

Ryker had something in him that made him *different*. If I told him to do something, he wouldn't ask questions. He would just do it. He would respect me. He cared about me. I knew the moment I laid eyes on him he was the one. I could just tell.

We all stepped onto the shore. The entire island had small stones circled around it. Every now and then a sign would say, *"This is where your journey begins. Decide whether or not you'll turn back here."*

"Well, this is it," I said. "Once I cross that line, The Stowaways would have officially set foot on Lost Island." I stood there, still wondering. Should we do this?

Ryker stepped forward and stood beside me. "Go ahead," he encouraged. "Don't think we're no different from the rest. They didn't have you leading them."

"Don't you think it's stupid, though?" I asked.

"No," he replied.

"But no one has ever made it out of here alive," I pointed out.

"Once again, they didn't have you," Ryker said.

"What difference..."

"Belle," Ryker took my hands and I turned towards him. "If someone offered you the chance to become a living legend, would you turn it down? No, you wouldn't. Go ahead."

I sniffled, about to cry tears of joy. Ryker tightly closed his eyes. I asked him, "What are you doing?"

"Trying not to look at you so that you won't cry," he answered.

"And I thought I'd seen it all," I giggled. "Don't let Sydney get to you. Come on."

I looked into the legendary island and took the first step.

The Unpredictable Island

We had been walking for about fifteen minutes. Ryker had to carry Alice because she was jumping into his arms every five seconds anyway.

Sydney suddenly screamed, "Spider! Spider! Get it off! Death! Black widow! Get it off of me! Help!"

"Death?" I asked as I picked up the very small black spider and flung it away.

"That was a... wait a minute. That wasn't a black widow. Um... silly me. Oh well, let's go," Sydney said with red cheeks.

"Sand pit!" Donna squawked.

"Do you mean quicksand?" Ryker asked.

"*Squawk!* No, I mean sand pit," Donna argued.

"No," Sawyer said. "I think you meant quick…aah!" Sawyer suddenly fell into a pit of quicksand! Ryker dropped Alice, grabbed the rope, and quickly tied it around his waist. Hopefully, he had acted fast enough. He handed me the rope.

"Don't let go. Bring me back up in fifty seconds," Ryker said just before he dived into the quicksand.

"It's so strange," Sydney said as she grabbed hold of the rope. "Quicksand isn't that fast, is it?"

"What if he can't get Sawyer? Will we just leave him? Does Ryker go back in? Is… is Sawyer going to die? Well, is he? Belle, answer me!" Alice sobbed. She and Sawyer were very close. He was like a brother to her.

"Alice, just stay calm and don't let go of the rope," I said. I was the captain. I had to stay in control.

"Is he going to die or not?" Alice demanded.

"I don't know, just do as I say," I stammered.

"It's been fifty seconds, pull him out," Sydney said.

142

We all pulled on the rope, but the sand seemed to harden the more we pulled. It was taking longer than we had expected. Were we going to be too late?

We eventually struggled and pulled Ryker out, who, sure enough, was holding onto Sawyer. They had barely made it out in time. Everyone threw their arms around them with joy, but that was only our first disaster.

A few minutes later I could hear Alice and Sydney talking.

"Why did you freak out back there?" Sydney asked.

"The Stowaways are the only family I've ever had," Alice answered after a while. "I can't afford to lose anyone, especially you and Sawyer. I was born in Salem, in the New World. For some reason, the Puritans considered red-heads witches, so they looked down upon my parents. They decided to get rid of me. After that, I was adopted twelve times and the same thing happened. People pity Ryker because one parent turned him down. *Twenty-six* parents turned me down."

"Alice, why have you never said this?" Sydney asked.

"I don't like to talk about it," she answered.

"Well, I want you to stay with me. I won't turn you down," Sydney promised.

Everything went smoothly after that... until something completely unexpected happened. We were walking through the island when the ground began to rapidly shake. The trees were falling all around us. We began to run to a clearer space, but it was hard to move across the shaking ground. Alice fell and I could hear a tree creaking. She froze. The tree began to fall.

"Alice, move!" I screamed as I ran in front of her and drew my sword. The tree fell over me and split in two. The earthquake stopped.

"Is everyone okay?" I asked.

"Belle, I think we should turn back," Sydney said.

"You're just saying that because you're a chicken," Ryker said.

"No. Something's wrong. Earthquakes and pumice scream 'volcano.' The earthquakes are just a pre-effect of an eruption," Sydney said with a worried voice.

"It's one earthquake," I said. "If you forgot, we're on Lost Island. If there are geysers, quicksand, and all that, then there are probably earthquakes, too."

"And volcanoes!" Sydney argued. "We are literally about to die if you don't get us off of this island *right now!*"

"Don't question me, Sydney!" I raised my voice. "I know you. You don't actually think that. You're too superstitious and you worry too much. Sorry, but it's true."

"I'm being smart!" Sydney yelled.

"You're being insecure," I said.

"Well, you're plenty insecure…"

"I'm also your captain!" I shouted. "Come with us or go back alone."

I began to walk, but Sydney did have a point. I stopped and conceded. "If another earthquake comes, we'll go back."

After about ten minutes the mood began to lighten. We came to a clearing with a small blue lake and other openings around it.

"Ooh! I think these are geysers!" Sawyer exclaimed. "Hey Ryker, wanna take a ride?"

"On the geysers? Can't that kill you?" Ryker asked.

"Nah," Sawyer claimed.

"Yes it can!" Sydney argued.

"Shut up, Sydney," Sawyer said.

"Now wait a minute!" Sydney shrieked. "You can't say that! You're nine!"

"Maybe we should listen to her. I mean, I'd rather not die," Ryker said.

"Oh, come on! It'll be fun," Sawyer begged.
"Yeah, but Sydney's smart," Ryker admitted.

"Oh, how flattering," Sydney muttered as she rolled her eyes.

"Flattering! Oh no! Belle, Ryker's cheating on you!" Sawyer yelled.

"No he's not," I objected.

"I'm not! Belle, I'm not!" Ryker panicked.

"Prove it," Sawyer teased.

"I will!" Ryker ran over to Sydney.

"Sydney, will you marry me?" Sawyer mocked.

"No, dummy," Sydney said as she slapped Ryker's face.

"Ouch! I was supposed to do that!" Ryker shouted before he slapped Sydney back.

"Propose to me?" Sydney demanded.

"No!" Ryker yelled.

Suddenly, tons of water burst out of the ground. It shot hundreds of feet into the air to make a beautiful masterpiece.

"Ryker, stick your hand in!" Sawyer exclaimed.

"Okay!" Ryker stuck his hand into the water and instantly jerked it back in anguish. The geyser stopped.

"It burnt me!" Ryker moaned.

"Oh my goodness! Are you okay?" I ran over to Ryker. His hand looked terribly hurt.

"Sawyer, if he'd jumped on that thing he would be dead right now! You could have killed him! You could be dead, too!" Alice shouted.

"I'm sorry! I didn't know!" Sawyer whined.

"Let me see," Sydney sighed. "Oh, this is really bad. Oh well. It seems you are about to die."

"What?" Ryker shrieked.

"You're not gonna die, you're just stupid," Sydney said.

"Ow! Don't touch it!" Ryker winced.

"You'll live. Do you want Sydney to help you or not?" I said.

"If you start crying, I'm gonna slap you," Sydney warned.

"I think one slap is plenty," I said.

"You're fine. Get up," Sydney dismissed him.

"You're not gonna do anything?" Ryker asked.

"Nope," I said," Let's go."

We went on walking and Sawyer suddenly stopped.

"Don't move," he said. The trees had seemed to make a tunnel. On the ground and coiled around the tree branches were all kinds of snakes.

"*Squawk!* Snakes! Yummy!" Donna exclaimed.

"You can't eat snakes," Alice said.

"Sure you can," I said. "I never have, though."

"Do we go around?" Ryker asked.

"Yeah, we have to," I said. Looking through the tunnel, I saw that one of the mountains was particularly close. There was a cloud around the mountain. It seemed to be hiding a dark secret. We went through the cedar trees, which were tightly packed together. The island was so strange to me. It was plotting something. I could just tell.

"Why can't we climb the mountain instead of going through it?" Alice asked.

"Three reasons," I said. "It's too dangerous, we need the key, and we don't know which one to climb."

We came out of the woods. The sun was going down.

"We can't travel in the dark," I said, "Let's get to a safer place and make camp."

"Wouldn't it be safer underground, away from the forest?" Sawyer asked.

"The center of the island is too far away," I said.

"What about this cave?" Ryker suggested. "It's completely empty."

"That'll do," I said. "Sydney packed some blankets. Come on."

After a few minutes, there were five small beds on the ground. A fire was going. After everyone had something to eat, we all went to bed. Sawyer and Alice were both afraid of sleeping in the dark on Lost Island, but we had to.

"Ryker, is it true that your father wanted to get rid of you?" I asked. "I'm just curious. You don't have to answer."

"It's true," he answered. "My mother turned me down before I was even born. My father only kept me because he didn't want to look bad. He hardly ever even spoke to me. He never said he loved me. I asked him sometimes, but he never had much of an answer. One day, he, all of a sudden, decides he is going to send me to boot camp. I refused. I knew he didn't care about me the least bit.

"One day, he took me to the harbor in London for a business trip. He left me outside and I found myself being chased by Jack and Jonathan. Not knowing what was going on, I left with you. I had no intention of going back. I wanted to run away. I had no idea who you were, but I wanted to go with you. You saved my life."

"I'm really sorry," I said. I had no idea his past had been that hard. I wanted to cry.

"Oh, don't be sorry. I'm fine now."

"Okay," I sighed, before I fell asleep.

Midnight in Lost Island

It was midnight. I woke up to Sydney screaming.

"What happened?" I asked, but the answer was clear. A huge brown snake was coiled on the floor at the cave's entrance.

"Sydney, did your hair get tangled or something?" Ryker asked, half-asleep.

"Or something," Sydney answered. "Look behind you."

"Why?" Ryker asked as he turned around. "Oh… a huge ferocious snake. How lovely."

"Move away from the snake," I whispered. Ryker crawled to the back wall of the cave. Sawyer, Alice, and Donna woke up and did the same.

"Is it poisonous?" Alice asked.

"No, I don't think so," Sydney whispered.

"*Squawk! Squawk!* Snake!" Donna squealed. I knew what she wanted to do. I didn't want her to make it angry.

"Donna, stop," I ordered.

"*Squawk!* Mean snake! Bad snake!" Donna flew over to the snake and perched on its head.

"Donna, come back. Come back. Don't do anything to the snake," I begged.

"*Squawk! Squawk! Squawk!* Bad snake! Leave! Leave!" Donna shrieked. The snake hissed and raised its head.

"Come back, Donna!" I whispered. The snake was already unhappy. Soon it would be too late.

The snake suddenly charged at Alice. It knocked over the lamp and Ryker's bed caught on fire. The exit was blocked. We were trapped. The snake wrapped itself around Alice's ankle and she fell. It was about to bite her neck.

"No!" Sydney screamed. She tried to kill the snake, but only wounded it. It hissed at her and charged. She kept aiming her sword at it, but it dodged. She was quick to move away from it when it tried to bite her. However, she knew she wouldn't last much longer.

Ryker, of all people, tried to help her. I helped, too, but told the younger kids to stay back. I eventually sliced the end of its tail off, but that only made it angrier... still at Sydney. I had weakened it, though.

"Alice, find the water," I said. She quickly searched through the bag. She couldn't find the water to put out the fire.

The snake quickly wrapped itself around Sydney. Before I could do anything, it bit her arm. Sydney fell back and cried and screamed. I had failed her!

"Alright, that's enough!" Ryker stormed and shoved his sword down the snake's throat. As the snake choked on the sword, I chopped its head off. It was dead. I dumped everything out of the bag, found the water, and put out the fire.

Sydney was in pain. I ran to her and tried to help, but she was crying so much she couldn't even talk and I didn't know what to do. When she barely managed to get the words out, I cleaned the wound and bandaged it. As I did, I relayed all of the reasons I was a failure and everything I had done wrong. I was angry at myself, so I had to find someone else to blame. Donna! I finished helping Sydney and became furious.

"You stupid bird!" I yelled. I grabbed Donna and clutched her angrily. Ryker grabbed me and pulled Donna away from me.

"Stop it!" he yelled. "What has gotten into you?"

"It's all her fault!" I screamed. "She's the one we went after when we were attacked. She's the one who ran away. She's the one who made the snake angry. She always ruins everything!"

"Belle, this isn't like you, what's wrong?" Ryker demanded.

"You called her stupid, too. You can't blame me!" I shouted, trying to get away from him.

"Yeah, well, I shouldn't have," Ryker said.

"It doesn't matter," I argued. "She's a parrot. It's not like she has feelings."

"You think it's *your* fault, don't you? You're just blaming Donna. Well, guess what. You always force me to tell you all of my crazy problems, so go ahead, start from the beginning!" Ryker said. Did he actually care that much?

I began to cry. "I'm an orphan. I was abused for ten years. Everything I do turns out really, really bad. Dylan told me to leave without him and now I don't know what they've done to him. I'm thirteen years old and I'm a captain. I'm supposed to be perfect. The Queen of England probably wants my head because I live on a ship and don't wear a dress every day.

"Who knows how many times we've almost died on this one voyage? I have to do everything right, but I can't. I want to try to find the treasure but it just seems stupid. And I feel like I have to be some sort of hero, which is obviously impossible."

"You *are* a hero," Ryker said. "To me, at least. I mean, you've probably broken the record for saving the most lives. Look, I was running from bandits, saw a really pretty girl, hopped on her ship, and I'm still alive."

"And madly in love at that!" Sawyer exclaimed. "This is getting quite romantic. Go ahead, you know want to."

"Want to… what?" Ryker asked.

"Kiss her!" Sawyer answered.

"Stop it," I said,. "Go. Shoo. Hey, Sydney, how's your arm?"

"It's fine," she said.

"Okay, I want to get into the underground passage as soon as possible. No more accidents. Let's pack up and go," I directed. We packed everything into the bag and left the cave. We traveled in the dark for a few hours. After a while, we came to another clearing. In the center there stood a tall pillar with a message engraved on it.

"Ryker, hand me the lantern," I said.

He handed me the lantern and I read the message:

This door will take you into the underground passage. You cannot retrace your steps if you go in. Chances are you will not make it out. This is your LAST CHANCE to turn back.

But I did not question myself this time. I opened the door on the other side of the pillar. "Come on," I said as we began to walk down...

The Underground Passage

The stairs came to an end. Just a few feet away was a cliff.

"What is this?" Sydney asked. "Are we supposed to just jump? No, no, no! I am not putting up with this! Let's just turn back. Alright, let's go!"

"There's a net down there," I mused as I peered over the cliff. "It is completely safe. Come on. I am not turning back because you're too scared. You'll be fine." I jumped over the cliff.

"Ryker, can I have the rope?" Sydney asked.

"Sydney, just jump," I urged.

"But I don't want to jump!" Sydney exclaimed. "I don't like heights!"

"*Squawk!* I do! I flew one hundred feet above the ocean one time. I even flew to the moon one time!" Donna bragged.

"Donna, no one has ever flown to the moon," Ryker said, "and no one ever will."

"That's not true at all!" Sydney argued. "Sure, it might not be until the Nineteen-Sixties or so, but it will happen."

"As if!" Alice retorted as she took the bag with the rope. "See you at the bottom!"

"She just... the rope... she..." Sydney stuttered.

"She just took the rope, and jumped with it," Ryker finished. "Hey, Sawyer, grab Sydney's feet and I'll grab her hands... that sounds wrong... I'll grab her feet. Swing her over."

"No! Stop! Don't!" Sydney panicked as she was picked up. "You can't do this! Wait! I don't actually think you're stupid and ugly! I was just joking!"

"Ladies first!" Sawyer said.

"One, two, goodbye!" Ryker exclaimed as Sydney fell onto the net. He and Sawyer jumped down after her.

"See, that wasn't so bad, now was it?" I said.

"Whatever," Sydney muttered.

"Great, let's go," I grinned.

The wall of the dead-end had a row of numbers on it that read:

$a(-3)=b \ b+47=32$ *What is a?*

"What even is this?" I wondered.

"That is algebra and I will let Sydney do it because I hate algebra," Ryker answered.

"I can see why," I said.

"Let me see," Sydney said. "Oh, this isn't so bad. Give me the paper and quill and ink."

"Here is a piece of paper and some ink," Sawyer said.

"And a quill," Sydney repeated.

"You didn't bring one," Alice said.

"I can't write without a quill," Sydney complained.

"Use your brain," I suggested.

"That's too hard," Sydney said. "I'll mess up."

"Donna, come here," I ordered.

"Why?" she asked.

"I need a feather," I said.

"Don't you dare!" Donna squealed.

"Hold still," I snapped.

"I don't like pain," Donna objected.

"Beauty is pain," I said as I kept tugging at a feather.

"I don't care!" she screeched.

"I'll give you cake," I said and Donna instantly froze. I gave Sydney the feather.

"Belle, Ryker, come here," Sawyer called with a grin.

"Oh no, what are you gonna do?" I asked.

"Belle, stand here," Sawyer instructed. "Ryker, right here, one knee. Alright, say the words."

"What? What words?" Ryker asked.

"Fine, I'll be you," Sawyer said. "Belle, I think you are brave and ridiculously attractive. I literally have dreams about you. Sawyer is concerned. Anyway, will you marry me?"

"Sawyer, you're a lunatic," I chided.

"Now give her the ring!" Sawyer exclaimed.

"You *are* a lunatic," Ryker agreed, dumbstruck.

"You didn't even get a ring?" Sawyer asked. "Wow, this is the worst proposal in all of the world's history."

"I didn't want to propose to her!" Ryker exclaimed. "Belle, forget any of this ever happened. Please!"

"Sawyer, give him a break," I said. "Don't you think Ryker's been through enough?"

The wall suddenly opened into another room.

"Five," Sydney announced. "The answer was five. Ryker, what's with that look on your face?"

"Nothing! Nothing! Everything is completely fine! Let's go," Ryker said as we all entered into the next room. There were columns going around the room getting taller and taller like steps and a hole in the ceiling.

"We go up," I said. "This looks easy. Come on."

We all began to climb the steps. I got to the last one and jumped through the ceiling. I almost tripped on a wire as I came out. Suddenly, I heard a rumbling noise as sharp blades began to come out of the ceiling. I then noticed dead bodies laying on the ground. The sight of them made me shiver.

"Belle, it smells like something died in here," Sydney complained and then looked at the floor. "Oh, that makes sense."

"Maybe someone could go around them," Alice suggested.

"I don't think anyone would fit through there. Nice try, though." I said.

"I can!" Donna declared.

"Yeah, but we can't," Sawyer said.

"She can just push that thing in the wall over there and shut it down," Ryker observed.

"Yeah," Donna squawked as she inched to the other side and shut down the blades.

"Cool!" Sawyer approved as he jumped across the bodies. I hoped most boys weren't like this. It was terrible... and cringy.

"Sawyer, please," I begged as I picked him up, "just try to be normal."

"That is normal, for Sawyer," Ryker said.

"Oh," I said. "Do you need your own room?"

"I want my own room!" Sydney exclaimed. "Do you know how many times Alice has tried to do karate and destroyed my bookshelf, or my desk, or my face?"

"Well, it's not my fault all of her stuff is in my way," Alice fussed. "Hey, Sawyer, did you know I'm taller than you?"

"Impossible! You're two years younger than me," Sawyer argued.

"No, she's six inches taller than you," Ryker said.

"I hate to break it to you, but you're short. Really short," I added.

The next room had a wall that was meant for climbing and strange dark tunnels in the ceiling. I went to the wall and began to climb. The moment I put my foot on one particular hold, it moved in. I clung to the wall and froze. Just then, a huge boulder fell from the ceiling! I flung myself to the side and it barely missed me.

"It's a trap," I warned, catching my breath, "Some of the holds aren't fully attached to the wall. You should be able to tell which ones are which. Sawyer, hop on Ryker's back. I don't trust you."

"Don't trust me?" Sawyer exclaimed.

"If I know you, you'll get us all crushed," Ryker said.

So we all cautiously climbed to the top of the wall. Alice was the last one to the top. She was almost up when she slipped and her foot barely missed one of the dangerous holds. I pulled her up and we continued. The next test was a riddle.

The man who sailed the ocean blue
Defied the ideas of his day.
Around the world 'til twenty-two
Gave it his all come what may.
He proved his theory, he needed to
But before the quest was over came the end of his days.

"Magellan," I said, "I heard tales of him when I was little. I guess you just push in the letters according to his name. M-A-G-E-L-L-A-N."

The door opened. The next room had a skeleton with its hands cupped.

"No way! It's a real skeleton!" Sawyer jumped around happily. *Cringe.*

"It's wooden, Sawyer," Alice pointed out.

"*Squawk!* Bones are made of wood. This is a dead guy," Donna stated.

"I shouldn't even try to tell her," Alice rolled her eyes.

"Alright," I said. "There are three stones. We put the wrong stone, and we die. Choose wisely."

"Okay, this is actually really easy," Sydney said. "The pebble is too light. The machine wouldn't even be able to tell it apart from nothing. That boulder would break the wood. Put the medium one."

"You can't let her decide," Ryker admonished.

"Do you have a better idea?" I asked, as I put the medium rock in the skeleton's hands. The wall opened.

"This machinery is amazing!" Sydney enthused. "I mean, the man is a genius. Not only an explorer but an inventor, too."

"I'd love to see Clark's face when we get our hands on that gold!" I said.

"Belle, you know when you were having that emotional breakdown, the tenth one this week, the one in the cave," Alice started.

"You have problems," Sawyer observed.

"You mentioned some guy named Dylan," Alice said. "Who in the world is that?"

"Your ex?" Sawyer teased.

"Oh my gosh, no," I answered," He's someone I knew..." My words were cut off. The ground began to shake. In fact, the whole room was rapidly shaking!

Another Fear and Another Doubt

I tripped and Sydney caught me, but I dropped the lantern. It shattered and went out. It was now too dark to see anything.

"Is everyone alright, no one's hurt?" I asked.

"Something touched me!" Alice screamed.

"It's just that skeleton," I said," Here, grab my hand."

"Does Ryker need to grab your hand?" Sawyer teased.

"Sawyer, not now!" Ryker advised.

"Alice, do you still have the bag?" Sydney asked. "The only other lantern we have is broken, but there's a torch and some matches."

Alice dug through the bag. "I can't find anything."

"Of course, you can't, give it to me," Sydney grunted.

"Where are you?" Alice asked.

"Here."

"Where is here?"

"Here!"

"Where?"

"Alice, give me the bag!" Sydney screamed, panicking.

"Sydney, chill," I said. "Alice, she's right here."

"Give me the bag!" Sydney bellowed as she snatched the bag and lit the torch. The shaking stopped. Ryker had a horrified look on his face.

"Ryker, are you okay?" I asked.

"Girls are so… dramatic," he answered. He looked hypnotized.

"Yes, you should know that by now," I said.

"That's why I'm staying single," Sawyer said with a grin.

Sydney looked even worse. She looked like she had come to realize something terrible.

"How do we know… How do we know we'll make it out… alive?" Sydney gulped.

"What makes you think we won't?" I asked.

"Logic. History. Science. I mean, shouldn't we be at least a little afraid?" she questioned.

"Not helping," Ryker mouthed at Sydney.

I nodded. I went to the corner of the room and sat down. The rest of the crew went on talking.

"Sydney, how could you say that?" Ryker whispered angrily.

"You think she's so strong, it's not my fault if she can't handle the truth," Sydney hissed.

"She's already upset. You just made it worse."

"Well, she shouldn't have even taken us here in the first place!"

"She is the reason most of us are alive, have you *met* her? It's obvious we're gonna make out of here, but that's pretty hard to believe when you're around. Do you ever know when to shut up?"

"Now, you've hurt her feelings before, too."

"I know that, but I was trying to protect her."

"Yeah, me, too."

"No, you're just finding things to worry about like you always do. She's been through a lot," Ryker sighed. "I wonder why you never had any friends at boarding school!"

No one said anything after that. Sydney didn't dare to speak. The room was silent. I was huddled by the wall crying and thinking.

I should have never taken the Stowaways here. Even before coming to Lost Island, our journey was going horribly. And although that was close to normal for us, I still felt terrible. I always knew we'd have our trials and tests on the island, but we were risking our lives. And for what? A bit of fun?

Not even adults could make it out of this place alive. I always thought we could do it, but I shouldn't have believed that. It wasn't logical.

No. No, it was impossible. Now there was only one way out; to keep going, which could never end well. We were trapped. I had made a terrible decision and instantly, all the lives of our crew were taken. To make things better, it was all my fault.

"You okay?" Ryker asked as he sat next to me.

"I'm perfectly fine. We're all about to die," I said.

"Now, I thought you were over that," he smiled.

"I was," I said. "That is, until I finally figured it out."

"Figured what out?"

"The fact that I'm just a stupid failure who can't do anything right."

"You don't actually think that."

"No, I do. I do. It's simple, really," I said as I stood up. "*I'm* the one who took us here. *I'm* the one who took us to Seaside Scalawags, where we lost Donna. *I'm* the one who took us into the passage, where we were all just about killed. *I'm* the one who took us to Shark Island. I could go on and on!"

"Don't." Ryker interrupted. "We're gonna get out of here. It just so happens Donna was afraid of the storm that night. We had to go into that passage, and nothing would have happened had Clark not been after you. At Shark Island, you didn't know better."

"Yes, I did…"

"Yeah, well, whatever. You forgot. What I'm trying to say is that you are absolutely not a stupid failure and we are all going to be fine."

"Prove it," I said.

"Look, Belle," Ryker reasoned. "*You* are the reason we're all here, together, right now."

"Therefore proving my point," I said. "*I* brought us here. *I'm* responsible…"

"No, not *here*. I mean we're all a crew, and alive because of *you*."

"Sure, I changed all our lives… and then ended them," I said, bitterly.

"You are very hard to work with," Ryker sighed, frustrated. "Hear me out. Every chance you got, you doubted yourself, except for the one we couldn't go back on. See, the whole time, you knew we'd make it out, you just think too hard about it."

"I was trying to be sensible," I replied.

"No, you just think that because Sydney's a jerk who never knows when to shut up."

"Sydney is looking out for us," I interrupted.

"No, she's just nurturing her own worries… big difference," Ryker said.

"I don't see much difference," I argued. "Sydney knows stuff. She's smart enough to know that there is a volcano somewhere on this island."

"Now, that's just silly."

"If it weren't for Sydney, we would all be dead right now. Why? Because she is the smartest girl alive and I know nothing because I grew up in a cargo hold! So why don't we go ahead and just make her captain?"

"If Sydney were captain, all of my nightmares would come true in one day," Ryker protested.

"Well, at least you'd all be alive!" I shouted and sobbed at the same time.

"None of us would be alive if it weren't for you, for the five hundredth time!"

"Well, someone else would have been better off if I were never born," I said.

"I have a hard time believing that, who?"

"No one."

"Alright, then," Ryker said," I'll just assume it's me."

"Not who I had in mind, but, then again, yes," I replied.

"And it's because…?"

"I'm not good enough for you," I said abruptly.

"Oh really?" Ryker asked.

"Yes, I guess I'll just have to spell it out for you, won't I? Well, alright then. Had I never come to that harbor, you would be happily living your life with your father in your mansion."

"I disagree!"

"Ryker, let me speak. But instead, I was so stupid and in love that I actually let you stay, holding you captive…"

"I wanted to stay!"

"And now you're here, about to die, because of me. Here's a life lesson: never get your hopes up and don't take chances on the only friends you've ever had." I began to cry again and sat down. "I feel like... I feel like I've been making the wrong decisions since day one. No matter how hard I try, someone always ends up getting hurt. And now we're stuck here, and it's all because of me.

"Listen, Ryker, you don't understand. I'm the captain, which makes me responsible. And even before I became captain, I messed up. I wouldn't even be alive if it weren't... if it weren't for..."

I was crying so hard that I couldn't even speak anymore. I had too many painful memories, too many mistakes, and too many worries. I couldn't handle it anymore.

Ryker sat down next to me. "I understand," he offered. "You had a hard past, and then you tried to run an entire pirate ship. You haven't done anything wrong. I mean, I admire everything you do. You're amazing and I am absolutely positive that Sawyer is eavesdropping right now.

"But anyway, you had done things that most girls your age don't even know how to dream of doing. Most girls your age are probably sipping tea with their legs crossed right now. You know, you can tell me, if you want to... whose life you 'ruined'... if it wasn't mine."

I stared at Ryker in tears. My childhood had been painful. I never wanted to think about it or tell anyone about it. But at this point, it was the only thing I could do.

After a while I said, "I wasn't alone on the *Cobra*. There was someone else with me. His name was Dylan, he was two years older than me, and he was the one who kept me alive for almost ten years. He gave me almost everything he had. He could hardly even take care of himself because of me.

"And then one day he said, 'Belle, it's about time you left this place. You need to go now,' and then he showed me a small rowboat I could escape on. I could see the island that I had gone to off in the distance.

"After I left, I could hear Captain Clark screaming at the top of his lungs at Dylan. I know he was punished horribly, all because he was trying to save me. And then the other night, at our fight in The Passage of Shadows, I saw him. He looked even worse. I didn't know how he was still alive. I just wish he could have taken care of himself, instead of me."

Ryker took my hand. "Hey, you don't have to feel guilty because someone tried their hardest to take care of you," he said, as he dried my tears.

"But now he needs help, and I'm not there. Someday, I'll have to go back for him, or else I'd never forgive myself," I said.

"Yes, maybe," Ryker agreed. "But not yet. You weren't ready in the Passage of Shadows. You were strong enough, but you weren't ready. And if this Dylan really tried that hard to keep you alive, it would only hurt him if Clark were to kill you. But we'll go back for him, I promise."

I smiled at Ryker. And for a moment I felt like someone who people looked up to, and I felt loved.

"*Squawk!*" Donna perched on Ryker's head. "You're not a loser or a failure. Leave that stuff to your weird husband. Ryker, did you know you're a dingbat? Well, you are. You can't just run away and get married because you got bored."

"But that's exactly what you did!" Ryker argued as he pushed Donna away.

"No, I didn't get married," Donna squawked.

"I didn't either, weirdo!"

"Ryker, can you kiss her now?" Sawyer asked.
"Sawyer, please, for crying out loud, stop making fun of us!" I laughed.

"Belle, it's not funny. Sawyer, go get your own love life," Ryker grimaced.

"Oh... okay then... Alice, come here," Sawyer called.

"Oh no," Alice protested as she jumped up. I wanted to cover my eyes. I should have, because right then and there Sawyer grabbed Alice's head and kissed her on the cheek! I gasped and closed my eyes.

"Sawyer, you are the most disgusting boy alive!" Alice shrieked before she slapped him across the face and kicked him in the shin.

"Wait, Alice, it's not like that, I was only trying to be cringy!" Sawyer wailed.

"Well, you sure are just that! Wow, what a great first kiss," Alice said sarcastically.

"Alright, that's enough," I said. "No more kisses, no more beating people up, and please, no more being cringy, Sawyer. Sydney, you should be throwing out sarcastic insults by now. What's your deal?"

"I'm a terrible brat who doesn't know when to shut up," she mumbled.

"You're starting to sound like me," I said.

"So what if I do?" Sydney asked.

"Don't beat yourself up. I forgive you, now let's go. Don't be a brat next time. It's literally that easy. Come on," I said and that was that.

The Hardest is Yet to Come

After solving a few more riddles and going through a few more obstacles, we decided to call it a night. Sydney had apologized at least fifty times before we could all go to sleep. I knew she felt terrible, but it was starting to become excessive, so I told her she was fine and forgiven and somewhat annoying, which finally got her to stop.

The next day, we continued our journey through the underground passage. We came to another puzzle with a sign saying:

You have made it far. You have yet only four stages left, but they will be the hardest. They will require bravery, strength, agility, and knowledge. Here is a hint to the next riddle:

A serpent of the strangest seas
Killed by the demi-god, Hercules

With many heads that hiss and bite
It shines in the sky across the night.

"Oh! I've got it! I've got it! It's a sea snake monster!" Ryker exclaimed.

"Ryker, that's not a thing," I said.

"Wait a minute, I think... no, no. I can't say this," Sydney started.

"Oh, no. You think Ryker's onto something, don't you?" Alice asked.

"Ha! I was right! It's a sea snake monster!" Ryker bragged, jumping up and down.

"It's a hydra," Sydney said, rolling her eyes. "Does anyone know what the whole *'shines in the sky'* thing is for?"

I looked at the wall, which had many small circles jutting out of it. They almost reminded me of the stars. Then I realized something.

"*The Hydra* is a constellation!" I cried and pointed to the wall. "These are the stars. I think if you push the right ones in, the door will open!"

Sydney's eyes widened and she grinned. She gave me a suffocating hug and screamed, "Belle, you're a genius! That's it! You did it! Yay!"

"Great, now let me go so I can breathe," I laughed and Sydney let me go. "Sawyer, come here. You know this stuff."

"Yes, so-called genius lady!" Sawyer acquiesced.

"Sawyer, I'm no lady, but whatever. Now, get over here. How much do you know about the *Hydra*?"

"Um… I think this is the head," Sawyer said.

"That's its tail," I corrected him.

"Oh, well, I'm bad at this. Belle, this is boring," Sawyer complained.

"Too bad. I just so happened to find one of the few things you know, so you are going to put up with it," I replied.

"What's in it for me?" Sawyer asked with a grin.

"We don't die in here," I offered.

"I'm gonna need a little more than that," Sawyer balked.

"I'll give you one-sixth of the treasure we find," I added.

"But isn't that as much as everyone else gets?" Sawyer asked.

"Just be quiet and help!" I barked, aggravated. I wasn't going to let Sawyer make a bargain with me. Three rules I always had on the *Pegasus* were: Don't take any advice from Sawyer, don't make any bargains with Sawyer, and do not, under any circumstance, give Sawyer too much sugar.

Ryker would often get caught breaking all three of these rules, and I was definitely starting to get tired of Sawyer brainwashing him with his 'therapy appointments'.

Time went by and after about fifteen minutes, we finished the constellation, but nothing happened.

"Why is the door not opening?" I puzzled. After a minute, I was so exasperated that I kicked the door, only to realize that it was made of solid rock. "Ouch! Bad idea! Bad idea! Ugh!" I shouted as I hopped around on one foot.

"*Squawk!* Stop acting stupid like your husband! You're obviously missing one," Donna reproved me.

"Oh, yeah!" I said. "It's that one, right, Sawyer? Sawyer, stop picking your nose and get over here!"

"Constellations are boring, count me out!" Sawyer resisted.

"Sawyer, stop being a crusty weirdo and help her!" Alice demanded. She grabbed his nose and pulled him towards me.

"Alright, which one is it?" I asked.

"I don't know," Sawyer claimed.

"Just answer the question," I sighed.

"That one," Sawyer decided.

I pushed in the missing star in the constellation and crossed my fingers. The wall opened. The next room had a very high ceiling and an obstacle course leading to the top.

"Me first! Me first!" Sawyer exclaimed as he ran towards the first obstacle.

"Nope!" I said as I picked him up. "You are way too clumsy to go anywhere without a rope."

"Ropes are for losers," Alice moaned.

"Yeah, ropes are for chickens, cowards, and scaredy cats," Sawyer agreed.

"Does she look like any of those?" Ryker asked.

"No, but *you* do," Alice muttered.

"That's so mean!" Ryker objected.

"Ryker, do you know why she doesn't look like a loser to you?" Sawyer asked. I knew he was about to make fun of Ryker, but I kept my grinning mouth shut.

"Because she's not one?" Ryker guessed.

"No. Well, yes. But no," Sawyer answered. "It's because when you look at her all you can see is her shining emerald eyes, and her golden hair dancing in the wind, and those beautiful red lips that you oh so badly want to…"

"Oh, my gosh! I am so done with you making fun of us!" Ryker shouted.

"Hey, chill," Alice said. "If you're gonna act like Sydney, do it with some respect! Now, I want you to pop your knee, stick out your hip, and snap."

"Absolutely not!" Ryker shot back.

"Well, then this sounds like a 'you' problem, not a 'me' problem," Alice decided, as she put her hand on her hip and fluttered her eyelashes.

"Sawyer, just put on the rope," I said.

"Whatever," Sawyer gave in. I tied a rope around his waist and tossed it over a beam near the ceiling. It should have been like a pulley or a belay system, but it was hard to pull the rope over the shaft. And then, the worst thing happened.

"Belle, what am I supposed to do?" Sawyer yelled.

"You're supposed to climb that net. Isn't it obvious?" I yelled back at him.

"Yeah, but it's not... *climby*," Sawyer whined.

"Sawyer, that's not even a word. 'Climby?' Really? Just go! My arms are getting tired," I said.

"Do you wanna switch?" Sydney asked me.

"Yes!" I exclaimed.

"No! No!" Sawyer screamed. "Not her! I don't trust her! She'll drop me! Please!"

"Oh, be quiet," Alice scolded.

Sawyer finally reached the top and figured out how to untie the rope. He threw it back down and Alice and Ryker got to go next. Sydney decided she would go last... she was probably stalling... and tied the rope around my waist.

I began to climb. The course really wasn't that tricky, but it worried me when I saw that the rope had gotten thinner from rubbing it on the beam. I made it to the top and tossed the rope down to Sydney.

"You look worried," Ryker said.

"Oh, I'm not good enough for you! Let's just make Sydney captain! Oh, my sweet ex, Dylan! Donna, you're stupid! The queen of England wants my head! I'm in love with Ryker, blah, blah," Alice teased.

"I don't sound like that!" I fumed.

"Actually, you do," Ryker ventured.

"What are you talking about?" I asked. I didn't know I was actually that emotional.

"You have problems," Sawyer stated.

"I do not," I argued, as I crossed my arms.

"Alright, then. What's happened?" Ryker asked.

"The rope's about to break and guess who's going next," I said quietly.

"Oof," Sawyer whispered.

"Hey, are you gossiping about me?" Sydney yelled from the bottom of the course. "Oh… um… Donna, it's your turn. Come on, let's put the rope around your waist."

"*Squawk!* I can fly, you dingbat!" Donna screeched.

"But, Donna, I'm stalling," Sydney begged. I had called it, knowing how Sydney was… well… Sydney.

"Oh, shut up," Donna squawked just before she flew up to me and perched on my arm.

"Sydney, come on!" I yelled.

"But- but- but… do I really have to?" Sydney stalled, avoiding eye contact.

"Start climbing!" Alice yelled.

"Okay, okay," Sydney groaned. "Sheesh. Ryker, why are you smiling like that?"

"No good reason," Ryker answered. Sydney began to climb. Once she got the hang of it, it was quite easy for her… until the rope finally broke. Sydney screamed as she caught the net that hung halfway through the course.

"Um, hello!" Sydney shouted. "I just about died and none of you looked the least bit concerned!"

"That's 'cause we're not," Ryker muttered.

"Help me!" Sydney shrieked.

"We can't, Sydney, the rope broke," I said.

"Then what do you expect me to do?" Sydney yelled.

"*Squawk!* Climb, dummy!" Donna answered.

"You're kidding," Sydney said, coldly.

"Sydney, you're wasting precious time, here. Because eventually, your arms will get tired and you'll fall and die," Sawyer said.

Everyone stared at him and I slapped him very lightly across the face. I didn't want to hurt a nine-year-old, but Sawyer was deeply annoying and almost an exception.

"Ouch! That didn't even hurt!" Sawyer mocked.

"I know," I said. "That was your warning slap. Stop being cringy."

"Sydney, hurry up!" Ryker yelled. "If you die, I'll have to put up with Belle crying for two months, and I don't think I can do that."

"Ryker, what did I just tell Sawyer? I'd slap you, too, but I can't really because of *certain things* I shouldn't say in front of these small children," I said, blushing.

"*Squawk!* Belle and Ryker sitting in a tree…"

"Okay, I guess I'll come up," Sydney said. "I want Easter lilies at my funeral and be sure to tell Michael that he has nice eyes."

"Alright, Sydney. Hurry up. They're starting to make fun of me and Ryker again," I yelled.

"I'm coming! I'm coming!" Sydney called out. She began to keep climbing and finally made it to the top. We came into a room with another riddle engraved into the wall reading:

What silently awakes you and doesn't let you sleep?
What is blazing hot with fire and many miles deep?
What keeps you in its grip and never lets you go?
What shines upon your day and puts light upon your road?

"I've got it!" Alice exclaimed. "It's Sydney! Because she sleep-talks about Michael all night and doesn't let me sleep."

"You literally just proved your point wrong," Sydney argued. "I'm not silent. The only thing that silently awakes you is light."

"Great, then. The answer is light," Sawyer concluded.

"Light does not put light upon your path," Ryker said.

"A lantern does," Sawyer said.

"Yeah, because this lantern, which is many miles deep, will hold you in its grip," I commented drily.

"So it's something big," Sydney said.

"Yeah, probably as big as the sun," Alice said. "Why are you all looking at me like that? It's not like I... Oh, it's the sun."

"The sun doesn't hold you in its grip," Ryker pointed out.

"Ryker do you know what gravity is?" Sydney asked sarcastically. "Well, it's that thing that is keeping us from floating off into space."

Sydney pushed in the letters on the wall before it opened to reveal the next room, which was huge. We were standing close to a ladder. We were almost out! But then I noticed the terrible, deep dark trench that was maybe fifty feet across. There was a rope tied to a lever and a sign next to it.

"Belle, come on," Sydney said. I continued to read the sign.

"What's that?" Ryker asked. "Guys, come on, over here."

Everyone crowded around that sign that said:

This is your last stage. It is merely a test of bravery. You can go out now, but you will not have the key. You will have to use the rope connected to the ceiling to swing across the pit and make it to the other side, where the key is. If you choose to take this risk, your entire crew will have to go with you, because once you remove this rope, you will trigger the doors to the other way out to seal shut. You will have to get across fast because I currently know something you don't know. From the moment you walk into this room, two blades will continue to slowly inch toward each other close to the ceiling and within an hour they will meet and cut the rope. Use the key to unlock the door on the other side. I wish you the best of luck.

"Well, are we doing this or not?" Sydney asked. I was shocked to hear her say that.

"What?" I breathed.

"I mean, come on. We put all this effort into our journey, it would be stupid to turn back now," Sydney shrugged.

"Okay, then," I said. "Ryker, I want you to go first so that you can help people when they get to the other side. I'll go last, just in case we run out of time."

"I didn't agree to this!" Ryker argued. "No, no, no! I am not letting you risk your life!"

"Ryker, I have the final say, now get ready, because your turn's first," I said.

"Fine, but you better not die at the last stage," he growled as he began to tie the rope around his waist.

"I won't," I replied but I truly was nervous. Ryker went ahead and swung across the pit. He thankfully made it to the other side and the rope came back to me.

"Sydney, you're next," I instructed.

"Nope."

"You're the one who wanted to do this so badly," I said.

"*Squawk!*" I can go next!" Donna chirped as she got ready for me to put the rope around her waist.

"Donna, you can fly," I reminded her. I tied the rope around Sydney's waist.

"Hurry up, Sydney!" Ryker yelled.

"Be quiet! I'm saying my prayers in case I die!" Sydney yelled back at him.

"Believe me, it's fun!" Ryker shouted. Sydney rolled her eyes. She took a deep breath, looked away from the terrifying drop, closed her eyes, and swung. She screamed at the top of her lungs until Ryker caught her. She wouldn't stop clinging to either him or the wall on the other side. Sawyer went next.

I was beginning to realize how long it was taking for one person to get the rope tied around their waist, to swing, and to take off the rope and return it. I started to worry. Alice would make it. I knew that much, but I was going last. I didn't really know if I would have time to go or not. I quickly got Alice ready to swing.

"Is something wrong?" she asked. Her voice seemed louder because of the echo in the cave.

"How much time do we have left?" I asked her, but the others could also hear me.

"Belle, we still have thirty minutes," Ryker yelled.

"Oh," I said, relieved. Maybe this would work after all. Why wouldn't it?

Alice swung and returned the rope to me. I didn't know why I was so worried. I felt like I was shaking, but

I knew we still had plenty of time. I tied the rope around my waist and prayed this would work. What was I so afraid of? Was it just me? Or could I just tell that something would go wrong? At this point, I was genuinely terrified. I knew I had to do this, and I swung. But when I did, something began to feel… off. Then, I knew what was wrong.

"It's another earthquake!" Sawyer screamed.

I hadn't been shaking before out of fear. Suddenly, one of the blades slid out of place and cut the rope. Because of the momentum I had, I was cast toward the others. Sydney leaped out to catch my hand. Our fingers slightly touched, but I was unable to grab her. I fell into the pitch-black chasm as Ryker grabbed Sydney while she was still within reach.

I really and truly was certain I would not survive the fall. Out of desperation, my hands felt the wall of the pit. I grabbed it and clung to it tightly. The jagged rocks had cut my arms and hands. I had also hit my head from landing there. I felt like I was about to pass out again, but kept gripping the rocks. It was too dark to see anything, but I could hear the Stowaways talking about what had just happened.

"Sawyer, get another rope out of our bag," Ryker yelled. Sawyer gave him a rope and he tied it around his waist.

"Ryker, what are you doing?" Sydney asked in tears.

"Saving her," he answered. "Isn't it obvious?"

"There's no one to save," Sydney cried.

"We don't know that!" Ryker snapped as he lit another torch.

"Ryker, she's dead," Sydney sobbed.

"We don't *know* that!" Ryker said again. "Hold this, and don't let go for any reason!" He handed Sydney the other end of the rope.

Sydney looked at Ryker with sorrow in her eyes. I finally realized what they were saying and screamed, "I'm down here! I'm alive! Help me, please!" Sydney was extremely shocked. She did something no one would have ever expected to see her do. She tied her end of the rope around her waist, snatched the extra torch out of Ryker's hand, and began her descent down the jagged wall.

"Belle, I'm coming!" Sydney yelled. "How far did you fall? Can you see anything?"

"No, it's too dark," I stammered. "I don't know how far I fell."

"Okay, that's okay. Just don't move," Sydney said. I looked up and my eyes could barely see a light maybe fifty feet above me. I wasn't going to die after all!

"Wait, I think I see you!" I yelled. I would have sounded happier had I not been in so much pain and the stakes weren't so high. A few minutes later I could actually see Sydney. She came down to where I was and reached out her hand.

"Come, on. Let's get out of here. You're gonna be okay," she assured me.

"Sydney, there's no way I can climb up there," I said.

"Well, what kind of a friend would I be if I had come all this way just to make you climb the whole way up yourself?" Sydney laughed as she tied the dangling rope around my waist to the one she had around hers. She yelled, "Alright, Ryker, pull us up!"

We began to rise higher and higher. I felt bad because I wasn't doing anything to help, but there was nothing I could do. Sydney tried to keep talking to stay calm. I didn't say much, though.

"You know, that cut on your right arm really doesn't look good," she went on. "I mean, I knew you may be a bit bruised and cut, but I never expected this. Do you feel okay? This may be worse than the other night with the *Cobra*. You don't think you're gonna pass out or anything, do you? You're not talking a lot. Tell me if something's wrong, okay?"

"I mean, yeah, I might pass out, but I don't really care about that right now. I just wanna get out of here," I answered her.

"Okay, do you think you can make it till we get to the top? It's just ten more minutes, and then I can help you a little more," Sydney said.

"Yeah, okay," I whispered. At that point, that was all I could do. After what seemed like hours, we finally reached the top of the cliff. Ryker pulled me up and I didn't let go of him for even a second, not after falling a hundred feet into that pitch-black void. That was the closest I had ever come to death, and I knew it, and I cried.

"I don't think she can stay conscious much longer," Sydney told Ryker. And at that, I closed my eyes and passed out...

The Secret is Out

After a few minutes, I woke up. Sydney was bandaging my arm and Ryker was doing whatever he possibly could to help me. They had always been good friends to me and I was thankful.

"*Squawk!* We found the key!" Donna sang as she perched on my face.

"Donna, why do you do this to me? Your claws hurt, like, a lot," I moaned.

"Talons! They're talons!" Donna corrected.

"Alright, do you feel okay? Do you wanna rest for a few minutes?" Sydney asked as she finished bandaging my arm.

"I'm okay. Thank you," I said.

"For what?" she asked.

"Saving my life. What else would I be thanking you for?"

"Oh, yeah, that. Well, that's what friends do," she said and hugged me.

"So, who's ready to get out of here?" I asked.

"Me!" Ryker exclaimed.

"It's a rhetorical question," Sydney grunted.

"Alright, I guess you all can just stay here," I goaded. "Ryker and I can dig up the treasure."

"That's not fair!" Alice whined.

"Well, none of you answered the question," I said.

"You're just favoring him because he's your favorite!" Sawyer complained.

"Since when is Ryker your favorite?" Sydney asked with a wink.

"He's not. He is, however, the only one who answered my question," I said.

"He is your favorite!" Sawyer scolded.

"Well, you don't see me dating *you*, do you?" I asked.

"Stop! I don't want to think about that! Gross!" Sawyer covered his eyes as if that would help.

"Okay, no one cares about the question. Let's go," I said. I took the key and pushed it into the wall. I turned it and a door opened in the wall and a blinding light shone from outside. I smiled as my eyes adjusted.

We all looked at each other and shared the same idea in our hearts: We had just done what no grown-up had ever been capable of. We were almost legends! We were so close!

We arrived outside and hiked up the mountain. It didn't take long and we didn't have to climb far. When we reached the top of the mountain, we couldn't believe our eyes. Engraved in the mountain's peak was a massive box with a small keyhole in the center!

"Well, I guess this is it," I said with a grin. "All we have to do now is unlock the vault, take the treasure, and go."

I stooped down and pressed the key into the keyhole, took a deep breath, and turned the key. After a few seconds, which seemed like forever, the top of the vault split apart at the center to reveal tons of shining gold, jewels, pearls, swords, jewelry, and many other treasures. Everyone gasped at the sight. It was absolutely magnificent!

"What have we here?" Ryker asked excitedly just before he jumped into the pile of treasure and began to examine everything in the vault.

"Hey, look, it's Pedro Fransisco's will!" Sydney exclaimed as she picked up an old but still in good shape piece of paper.

"Let me see! Let me see!" Sawyer jumped around Sydney trying to get her attention as she read the will and put it safely away in the bag, still ignoring Sawyer.

"*Squawk!* Is there anything in there for me other than that stupid husband of yours?" Donna asked.

"Yeah, there's this perch made out of solid gold with gemstones engraved in it," Ryker said.

"I want it! I want it!" Donna squealed. Sydney put the perch in the bag and kept filling it with other things she found. She then pulled a huge tote out of our bag and held it up.

"Okay, guys, there's no possible way we can fit a bunch of treasure into our tiny bag, so I brought along something a bit bigger. Knock yourselves out," she told us.

"Hey, it's another piece of paper," Sawyer said as he held up a note. "Ec-hec-hem…"

"What kind of a sound is that?" Ryker asked.

"I was clearing my throat," Sawyer scoffed.

"That's not how you clear your throat!" Alice declared. "Watch…"

"Oh, no! Not this again!" I interrupted. I took the note from Sawyer's hand and read:

Congratulations! You have found my treasure and done what no one else can do. Inside the vault, you will find a captain's hat. Notice it fits you, for most are far too big. You see, when I planned this whole thing out, I knew it would be children who would succeed.

Adults may be bigger and stronger, but the only ones willing to take this risk would be pirates. That would not go well for them, because most pirates are mean, greedy, and honestly, they're not very bright. Children, however, can be both smart and brave. Now, if this is some band of pirates that's entirely kids, I'm sure you're not rude, crude, and stupid. All this to say, you are my new heirs. Well done.

"Found it!" Ryker announced as he held up an undersized captain's hat.

"Let me see," I said. He gave me the hat and I put it on my head. It fit me perfectly!

"Here, Belle, I can put that in our smaller bag if you want," Sydney held out her hand.

"Yes, please," I said. "Ryker, what's that in your hand?"

"Probably the diamond," Sawyer answered. "I'll bet you everything I own he's gonna make you a wedding ring out of it."

"Nice try, Sawyer, he's thirteen," I said.

"Yeah, well, Tutankhamen married a seven-year-old girl when he was nine," Alice said.

"Hmm, Alice, how old are you?" Ryker asked. I could tell that he would burst out laughing the moment Alice came to realize the awkward problem that had just occurred.

"Seven, duh," she replied.

"And how old is Sawyer?" I asked.

"Nine," Alice said.

"Oh no," Sydney giggled.

"What?" Sawyer asked, and then his eyes widened," Oh no! No! No! No! No! No!"

I finally needed payback, so I started chanting," Alice and Sawyer sitting in a tree, K-I-S-S-I-N-G…"

"We can't date! She's like my sister!" Sawyer argued.

"Great, now everyone here has been in a relationship except me," Sydney pouted.

"Boys are so overrated," Donna squawked.

"Says the one who ran away and got married," I teased.

"*Squawk!* That's exactly what *you* did," Donna returned.

"Donna, I'm not married, and I won't be for a long time," I explained for the five hundredth time. Donna tilted her head in confusion. She really didn't seem to understand the difference between dating and being married, but I gave her some slack because she was a parrot who almost married a French narcissist.

We continued to stuff the other bag with treasure, but then something happened that no one would have ever expected, but had still been warned of. The ground began to shake, but this didn't feel like any ordinary earthquake.

"Everyone just hang tight, it'll be over in a minute," I yelled, but my words had no comfort in them. The earthquake only became worse. The shaking became more rapid. The air became hot and the constantly denied thought forced itself into my mind.

"Sydney," I said, my voice trembling, "I think you were right all along."

"Wait," Ryker said. "You don't mean…"

"Yes. Yes, I think the volcano's erupting!" Sydney gasped. Everyone stared at her in shock.

"Which one…" I asked, but my words trailed off because I already knew the answer. I could tell by the look in Sydney's eyes. I knew it when she was exaggerating, and she had been all this time, even she was shocked to be right.

This was a look far worse than any I had ever seen, aside from a few other life-or-death situations. Her eyes didn't say 'life-or-death situation' though. They simply said, '*We're done for*'.

Flight, Sacrifice, and Tragedy

After a few long seconds my mind shifted back into reality and I suddenly ordered, "Run! Come on, we have to get out of here now!"

"My foot's stuck!" Ryker yelled. His ankle had been caught on a loose nail in the vault. Everyone struggled to free him, but it was a lost cause.

"How much time do we have left?" Alice asked with worry.

"Um… I don't know… not much… maybe forty-five minutes," Sydney answered.

"What?" I screamed. I began to pull his arm even harder.

"Yanking my arm off won't save us any time," Ryker said. "You guys go and find a way that isn't blocked. I can free myself."

"Sydney, take the others and find a way out, I'll help Ryker. Go!" I ordered.

"Why is this so hard?" I asked helplessly.

"I don't know, just let me do it so you can go help them," Ryker said.

"Well, what if you die or something and I don't know about it?" I asked. "I'm staying, they'll be fine."

"Belle, I'm not gonna..." The mountain's peak suddenly caved in and the vault fell with it. I grabbed Ryker's hand and the loose nail let go of his ankle.

"See, aren't you glad I stayed?" I yelled as I pulled him up.

"Yep, let's go!" he said. We began to cautiously, but also very quickly, run down the mountain. Not long after, I heard Sydney scream for help. I tried to move faster, but the mountain was too steep. I tripped and fell and rolled down the mountain, which actually proved to be faster. Ryker ran after me and met me at the bottom of the mountain.

"Belle! We're over here!" Sydney said as she came out from behind a few trees. "This was the only path we found, but come see."

We followed Sydney into the woods and found the same tunnel we had come to a few days before. It was covered in snakes, in the trees, on the ground, and everywhere else. There was no possible way any of us could have made it through without being bit by one.

"There's no other way out?" I asked.

"No, this is the only way," Alice sighed.

"Donna already flew back to the ship," Sawyer informed us.

"There's no way we could get through there. We're trapped." Sydney sounded weak. I could tell she was very uneasy and very anxious, but there was nothing I knew to do.

"If one of us went through with a sword, they might just be able to take out enough of the snakes to get the others through safely," Ryker suggested.

"Do you see that snake in the back? The golden one? Yeah, that's a golden lancehead snake, and it will kill you if it bites you! So, find another way out," Sydney argued.

"Sydney, there's *not* another way out!" Ryker declared.

"Whoever goes in there alive doesn't come out alive," Sydney retorted. "If you tell someone to go in there, you are jeopardizing their life."

"Then I'll jeopardize mine," Ryker said hesitantly.

"Ryker, no. No. No, I will not let you go in there, risking your life! Let me go instead," I ordered.

"No, I'll do it. I'm not taking any chances on you guys," Ryker insisted.

"No! No, you can't. I won't let you!" I declared, but I was beginning to cry.

"Belle, you have saved our lives many times. It's my turn," Ryker said.

"But you'll die!" I cried. "There's no possible way you'll make it out of there. Don't you realize that if you were to do this, you would be sacrificing yourself?"

"I'd sacrifice myself for this crew any day," Ryker said. It was plain and obvious that there was nothing I could ever do to persuade him out of his decision, but I kept trying anyway.

"But I don't want you to go in there. What about me? What about what I want? What if..."

"Do you trust me?" Ryker asked quietly.

"Yes," I said at length.

"Then let me do this," Ryker said. That was when I really and truly realized how little control I had in this situation. Ryker was about to sacrifice his life for the Stowaways, and there was nothing I could do to stop him.

"I love you," I sobbed. I knew a thirteen-year-old would not normally say that, but I didn't care. I did love him, and I was about to lose him.

"And I love you," he said. "Now, I don't want you running after me or anything like that. I just want you to get to the ship and get the others safe. They need you. And if I don't make it out, I don't want you going back for me, because if this crew doesn't make it out of here, what I'm about to do will turn out to be in vain. Do you understand?"

I nodded with tears.

"Sydney, make sure she doesn't try to come after me," Ryker said gruffly. The he looked into my eyes as though we were saying 'goodbye'.

Ryker took a deep breath. He knew how high the stakes were for everyone, especially for himself. He looked back at us and then ran into the tunnel of snakes. My heart dropped.

"Ryker, stop! Come back! No! Stop! Come back! Ryker!" I pleaded.

I tried to run in after him, but Sydney grabbed me and held me back. My soul was screaming so loudly that I couldn't scream myself.

Just when I thought things couldn't get any worse, the lancehead snake shot across Ryker and he fell to the ground and wailed in pain. The depths of my very heart throbbed in anguish.

"Belle, come on, we have to go!" Sydney urged. I stood there, frozen. Again Sydney said, "Belle, let's go. Belle, we have to go now! Come on!"

Sydney grabbed my arm and dragged me away from the snakes, from the volcano, and from Ryker. I suddenly stopped and shouted at Sydney, "What, you're just gonna leave him? No, we have to go back!"

"We don't have time," Sydney snapped. "He told us not to go back for him. Remember? Come on, we have to go!"

"*Really*, Sydney?" I was yelling. "You think I'm just gonna walk away from him and let him die here? I know what he said. I don't care! I'm going back."

"Well, then, let me help you!" Sydney begged.

"No, go get Sawyer and Alice to safety," I ordered,. "How much time do we have?"

"Thirty minutes."

"If I'm not back in thirty minutes hoist the sails and get away from here."

"But there's no wind. The only way we can get out fast enough is when the explosion happens. If the sails are up, we might could get away in time."

"Okay, move!" I barked. Sydney and I ran our separate ways, my way going toward the danger. Usually, a girl wouldn't be doing all the rescuing, but I was the one who had to save Ryker. He had fallen onto a jagged rock and his forehead was covered in blood. I struggled to pick him up and began trying to run toward the *Pegasus*.

It was scorching hot outside, I was sprinting, and I was straining to carry someone. This was torture. I felt as if I couldn't run any farther, and it didn't seem humanly possible. I went on like this, in agony and pain, struggling to breathe, for twenty minutes.

Every step brought more misery and every minute brought more worry. I couldn't even think straight, because the only thing on my mind was getting to the

Pegasus. I finally came to the edge of the island, but there was no possible way to get across the rocks. It was hopeless.

"Belle!" Sydney screamed. She jumped off of the ship and made her way toward me.

"Sydney, what are you doing? Get back onto the ship!" I said.

"I'm helping you, duh," Sydney said sharply. She grabbed Ryker and the two of us hurried across the strange floating rocks. It only became harder to breathe as the volcano went on and on spitting out poisonous fumes. The air became even hotter and steam was even coming from the water. Huge clouds blocked out the sum. Time was running out. Sydney finally gripped the rail of the ship and pulled the three of us over.

"Now!" Sydney screamed. And at that moment all of the sails went up in unison and the volcano erupted. Lava spewed out from its peak and dark clouds filled the sky.

The deadly winds blasted through the air, sending the *Pegasus* out to sea and almost tipping it over. I closed my eyes and gripped a rope. Was this the end, after all we'd been through? Would we be swallowed up by the scorching hot fumes? Would our journey have been in vain? Everything happened so fast. The ship went far out to sea and I didn't move an inch. Even after we had stopped, I stayed huddled on the deck hanging on to the rope.

"We're alive!" Alice proclaimed. "Belle! Get up! Get up! We're alive!"

I let go of the rope and saw that Lost Island was a safe distance away, but that gave me no relief. I immediately demanded, "Sydney, is Ryker okay?"

"I don't know," she admitted. "I'll see what I can do. All I can say was that he was bit, and the snake was venomous."

"He's not gonna die, is he?" Sawyer stammered.

"Well," Sydney said slowly, "I really don't know."

A Long Journey Just to Fail

I had been crying and worrying and praying in my room for hours when Sydney came in. I could tell by the expression on her face that something was terribly wrong.

"Well," she said, her voice shaking, "Ryker has broken one arm and two ribs… and his forehead was cut pretty badly… and he still hasn't woken up…" Sydney was about to say something else, but her words were interrupted with tears.

"Sydney? Sydney, what's wrong?" I asked. I knew what she might say, but I didn't want to believe it.

"I don't think Ryker's okay," Sydney confessed, wiping the tears off of her face.

"What do you mean? Of course, he's okay," I countered, denying the truth and knowing it, too.

"No," Sydney said. "Belle, I… I think he's dying.

"That's not true," I spat in anger. "No, it can't be true."

"It's true."

"No. No, you're lying!"

"Belle, I wouldn't lie to you."

"Ryker is not dying! That is the only truth there is!" I yelled.

"That's not the truth, that's just what you want," Sydney reasoned.

"Well, what makes you think you're so right, anyway? Because you're not!" I screamed.

"Just listen to me!" Sydney begged.

"No! I won't listen to you!"

"Please!"

"Shut up! Just shut up and go away! Get out of my room! Leave me alone!"

"Fine, then." Sydney gave up. "Oh, and just so you know, Sawyer and Alice don't know any of this. I didn't think they could handle it. I thought you could. I was wrong."

Sydney walked away, closing the door behind her. I thought to myself, "No, Ryker's not dead. He would never leave me behind. That would be too cruel. He wouldn't do that to me, knowing I can't live without him. Ryker will wake up any minute now, and everything will be okay. He's not dead. Sydney's wrong. Ryker's not dead.

"It's Sydney's fault all of this happened anyway. She knew the volcano would erupt. She could have gotten us out of there. It's her fault. She always hated Ryker, she wanted to kill him. Well, she failed, because Ryker's not dead. But she wants me to believe he is. He's not, though. But Sydney did try to kill him.

"Wait a minute! Belle, what are you saying? Sydney would never kill Ryker! *You* killed him! You led the Stowaways into Lost Island and there he died. It was your fault! Ryker is dead and it's all your fault. You failed, Captain Belle Smith! You came all this way just to fail."

I believed my words, and my heart shattered. My heart was too broken to cry, too broken to be sad, and too broken to feel anything. I just sat there, frozen.

It finally became real to me that Ryker was actually dying, and I wrestled with my cruel thoughts: "Why would he do this to me? He knows I can't live without him. He knows it! He really doesn't love me! If he did, he wouldn't have left me. He only wants the worst for me! Why would I ever have trusted him? He hates me...

"Belle! What is *wrong* with you? He sacrificed his life for you! He died in your place out of love. He loves you! You don't pity him. You're only pitying yourself!"

I let my tears fall freely. "He's dead. He died, and he was so sure we'd make it out alive. He believed in you, and you failed him. You should have gone in his place. But he didn't give you a choice. He still can't order you around. You should have gone in his place, but you didn't. You're selfish. You're selfish and a killer!

"But you're *not* a killer because Ryker's not dead! He's *not* dead, and you know it. Sydney's just being paranoid. She's always paranoid. But she is skilled in medicine and she's very smart, so maybe she is right. She *can't* be right though, because Ryker's not dead. He just isn't awake. He will wake up soon. He didn't die in Lost Island. No, no. He would never hurt you like that. But he *would* be hurting you if he didn't go in there. You could have died."

I let out a jagged sigh. "Ryker did die, then. He died and it's my fault. But I just can't believe he's dead. No, I'll deny it as long as I can. I'll go check on him and see for myself. He's just fine."

I got up, weary with battling these opposing thoughts. I found Sydney and asked, "Where's Ryker?"

"He's in his room. Sawyer's not in there," she added.

"I'm going to check on him," I said.

"Belle, he's not gonna wake up…" Sydney began.

"You don't *know* that!" I snapped, pushing past her. I opened the door to Ryker's room. He just laid there, not moving.

I sat down next to him. I held his cold hand, whispering, "I miss you. I love you, too. More than most anything. Please come back. Don't leave me like this. You don't deserve to die. Especially not you. You saved my life. You saved all our lives. You're a hero. I wish you could have known that. I really do love you. I'll always love you."

After that, I couldn't even speak anymore. I was choked with tears. Before I knew it, I was sobbing so hard that it was difficult to breathe. I had lost the boy I loved so dearly, and I blamed myself. I was miserable. But just then, I heard a voice and a small spark of hope burned in my crushed heart.

"Belle?" he asked, but my hope faded away when I looked up to see that it was Sawyer.

"Yeah," I said, wiping my face.

"Are you okay? You don't think Ryker's dying, do you? Sydney said he'd be just fine," Sawyer said.

Sydney had lied to him, but I also didn't want to give him the correct answer. He had already lost his family, and Ryker was the closest thing he had left. All I said was, "Don't you worry. Everything's gonna be alright. Go on and play."

"But I don't wanna play. I wanna stay here," Sawyer said.

"No, no. I think it'd be better if you didn't," I said, patting his shoulder.

"Oh… okay," Sawyer mumbled as he left. After he closed the door, I kept on crying and crying. I felt as though I had lost all hope and could never find a substitute for it. I needed Ryker, but he was gone now. I felt lost without him.

I knew I had Sydney, but she didn't always know how to help or understand me. Ryker usually listened to me and he usually had something good to say. I didn't think I could ever let go of him. And I went on crying and crying for a while.

"God, why did you take him from me?" I whispered. And at that, I fell into a hopeless despair. There was no denying it now: Ryker was dead.

No More Tears

I kept crying and grieving in my misery for hours. And again, I heard a voice.

"Belle?" he said softly. I knew it was just Sawyer again.

"What do you want?" I sobbed.

"For you to stop crying," he said. I looked at the door and Sawyer wasn't there. I realized that it was Ryker speaking.

"You're... alive?" I gasped.

"You bet," he said, sitting up. I suddenly threw my arms around him and wept.

"I thought I'd killed you," I sobbed.

"How in the world could you possibly think that?"

"Well, I was the one who led us into Lost Island, and then we almost died multiple times, and... and then I should've gone into that snake tunnel thing... whatever it is, in your place, but I didn't, and..."

"Did you make the volcano erupt?" Ryker asked.

"No, but it's still my fault. I lead you in there."

"But everyone told you to lead us into there, and you wanted to, and had it not been for that volcano we would have all been fine."

"Oh," I said in a small voice.

"So, it's not your fault, and we're the first-ever pirate crew to make it out of Lost Island alive," Ryker declared.

"Yeah... yeah, that's right!" I exclaimed, wiping away my tears. "We are, aren't we?"

"Yep."

"But how are you alive?" I asked. "Didn't you get bit by the death snake thing... whatever Sydney called it?"

"No, I tripped on another snake and fell," Ryker answered.

"But you passed out, and your hands were cold."

"I didn't pass out. I was knocked out from busting my head open. And my hands are always cold."

"But Sydney told me you were dying," I said.

"Is Sydney ever right?" Ryker asked.

"Yes," I answered.

"Well, she was wrong this time," Ryker assured me.

Suddenly, the door burst open, and in came Sydney. She stooped down and slapped Ryker in the face.

"You scared me! Shame on you!" she scolded.

"I saved your life," Ryker said casually.

"And you also made Belle go mentally insane, and you gave me a heart attack!" Sydney continued.

"You were concerned? Wow, that's a new one," Ryker replied.

"Of course, I was concerned," Sydney said as she rolled her eyes.

"Ryker, you're alive! Yay!" Alice exclaimed as she, Sawyer, and Donna rushed in through the door and jumped on top of Ryker to hug him.

"Hey, get off of him! He just broke two of his ribs and his arm!" Sydney scolded.

"Why do you sound concerned about that?" Sawyer asked, getting off of Ryker.

"Because we're friends," Sydney answered.

"*Squawk!* Cheater, cheater, pumpkin eater!" Donna chirped.

"Okay, okay. Acquaintances," Sydney said.

"Better," Alice said.

"Hey, remember the time Belle tried to claim that she and Ryker were just friends?" Sydney teased.

"We were!" I insisted.

"Yeah, totally," Alice said, rolling her eyes.

"Can you feel the love tonight?" Sawyer sang. "The peace the…"

"Yeah, 'cause you and Alice are *just friends*," I interrupted.

"Hey! That's not nice!" Sawyer whined.

"Nobody likes a hypocrite," Ryker said.

Donna flew to the bag we had carried throughout our journey and began to peck at it.

"Donna, what are you doing?" I asked.

"*Squawk!* I want my golden parrot perch!" Donna answered.

"Wait a minute!" I exclaimed before running to the bag and opening it. "We made it out alive and with treasure!"

"Ooh! We're that guy's heirs!" Ryker announced.
"He has a name," Sydney scoffed.

"Pedro Francisco," Sawyer declared.

"Okay, let's see…" I said. "The perch is for Donna. The hat is mine. Um… the will and the note I can frame somewhere. Ryker, you can have this spyglass. And the rest is just some jewels and coins and stuff that you can divide amongst yourselves."

Everyone came and rummaged through the treasures and kept the ones they wanted. Sydney kept all of the rings, bracelets, necklaces, hair pins, and earrings. Alice took a dagger and most of the jewels. Ryker kept his spyglass and also kept some of the coins. Sawyer found a sword and kept the majority of the coins and an eye patch that he had no need for. After there was nothing left to take, Pedro Francisco's will and his note were framed so everyone could see them.

After everyone had had something to eat, we all went to bed. Tired as I was, my excitement kept me awake. We had done it. We were the heirs to the Portuguese explorer and we were the legendary pirate crew who made it out of Lost Island alive and with treasure.

I had nothing to worry about anymore. The journey was over and successful. I kept reminiscing about the voyage in my mind and finally drifted off into sleep.

Another Voyage Awaits

"Belle! Belle! Wake up! Wake up! Wake up!" Alice demanded as she shook me awake.

"Alice! Leave her alone!" Sydney scolded.

"Belle, we have a surprise for you. Please get up. Please?" Alice begged.

"You're being rude. Let her sleep," Sydney pleaded.

"Are you even awake?" Alice asked as she forced my eyes open.

"What?" I asked, oblivious to anything the girls had just said.

"We have something for you, but it really can wait. And *someone* decided to get up early today," Sydney explained.

"Oh," I grumbled. "Hey, can we talk about this later? I'm still asleep."

"Well, everyone's already awake," Sydney said.

"But the hammock is comfy," I argued.

"Hm… maybe she needs what Sleeping Beauty needed," Alice suggested.

"Alright," Sydney grinned. "If you don't get up, we'll make Ryker kiss you."

"Sydney, that's not a threat," Alice argued. "That's a reward. Belle, if you don't get up, we'll make *Sawyer* kiss you. You know, the boy that picks his nose and eats it!"

"I'm up!" I exclaimed, stumbling out of my hammock.

"Great," Sydney said. "We'll leave. Come out when you're dressed."

After they left, I changed into the outfit I normally wore. I braided my hair like usual and came outside and discovered, to my astonishment, we were docked in a harbor in London!

"*Squawk!* Surprise! Surprise! Welcome to Africa!" Donna chirped.

"Africa, as in London," Ryker corrected.

"Oh! This is my surprise!" I exclaimed. "I hope we don't get killed or arrested or anything dumb like that. Otherwise, this is amazing!"

"Ryker says London has cake and other cool stuff," Sawyer cheered.

"Yes and certain brats who don't know when to shut up at boarding school," Sydney mumbled.

"What was that, Sydney?" I asked.

"Nothing," she answered quickly.

"Oh! I know what's in London!" I gushed as I jumped up and down. "Michael!"

"Ooh, Michael, your sweet sweetheart," Sawyer teased.

"Hey! It's not funny!" Sydney protested.

"I know," Ryker said. "I'm sure you hate having to be single for the rest of your life. And you'll die alone…"
"Shut your mouth!" Sydney shouted.

"Sydney, babies are too young to hear such words," Alice joked.

"Besides, you can't be mean to me. I saved your life," Ryker scolded.

"Well, you kinda had that one coming," I admitted.

"Belle, you, too? How could you?" Ryker sulked.

"Alright, fine," I said as I rolled my eyes. "No more making fun of Ryker. Even though you guys are hilarious and pretty accurate, Ryker's done a lot for us and I respect that." Ryker and I both blushed a little.

"Ooh! Belle's flirting with her boyfriend," Sawyer said before he stuck his tongue out.

"Let's just go," I said as I disembarked the ship. Everyone followed behind into the harbor.

We spent the rest of the day in London, getting suspicious looks the entire time. Sydney begged us to go dress shopping so that we would blend in more, but I refused. Wearing a dress simply went against everything I stood for. However, it was still a good day.

Sydney bought new canvases, paints, and sketchbooks along with more jewelry using her share of the gold. Sawyer, for some reason I didn't want to know, bought books on therapy and magic tricks. He claimed he was actually going to read them, but I had a hard time believing that. Sawyer wouldn't read to save his life.

Donna constantly reminded me of how I had promised to give her cake back in Lost Island. So, the six of us met up at a bakery near the harbor. After we got Donna's precious seven-layered cake, we made our way back to the *Pegasus*. We soon boarded the ship, but as I was about to lift the anchor, Sydney stopped me.

"Wait! Wait!" she exclaimed. "I have to find someone. I'll be right back!" Sydney ran back down, and toward the city.

"Belle, go and put on your hat," Alice said.

"Yeah, you just go in your room and close the door so that you can't see us," Sawyer said. "And believe me. This is not a prank."

"Oh, okay," I said as I went into my room. I knew Sawyer and Alice were up to something, but I played along. I found the hat and put it on in front of the mirror.

As I did, I realized how changed I suddenly felt. I didn't feel like I was alone or not good enough anymore. I finally felt like there was some worth to me, like I had finally done something right. I finally felt confident in myself, and loved, and looked up to. I didn't feel like a burden anymore.

All this time I had lost my confidence because I hadn't believed in myself. My friends had believed in me, but I hadn't believed in myself. But all the time we were on Lost Island, I had done something to be proud of. I had avoided giving up. And I was content with that.

I continued to stare into the mirror, but I suddenly heard Ryker shriek, "Belle! Help! This seven-year-old is attacking me! Help!"

I darted out of my room to find Alice pinning Ryker to the ground and Sawyer trying to give Ryker pigtails. I suddenly collapsed laughing.

"Hold him down!" Sawyer demanded.

"Belle, why are you laughing?" Ryker shouted. "Help me!"

"Sorry, honey, I'm too busy making fun of you," Alice mimicked.

"Just give me a second, I think I'm dying!" I gasped, barely able to even speak, much less breathe. As much as I wanted to help Ryker, this was hilarious.

"She is officially broken," Alice decided.

"He asked me! He asked me!" Sydney exclaimed as she ran up to the *Pegasus* and boarded it, stopping to demand, "What did you do to Ryker's head?"

"His hair just… Ryker, stay down! His hair was just a little pathetic, so we made a few changes," Alice answered meekly.

"Belle, you can't date this!" Sydney laughed.

"Yep, sure thing, Sydney," I said sarcastically," Okay, let him go."

Sawyer and Alice sighed and let Ryker go.

"Now, Sydney, what were you trying to tell us?" I asked.

"Michael asked me to the Royal Ball in November!" Sydney exclaimed as she bounced around and clapped her hands with joy.

"Oh, Sydney, that's great!" I said.

"I know!" Sydney happily agreed.

"Well, how about you guys go and do something away from here, like far away, like where you can't hear us. I wanted to talk to Belle... alone," Ryker said as he looked at me. I blushed and smiled at him. The others winked at us, then left us alone.

"Much better," Ryker said. "Okay, I wanted to give you this without Sawyer making fun of us." Ryker put his hand in his coat pocket.

"Wait," I said. "I'm pretty sure the others might be eavesdropping."

"Oh, right," Ryker said. "Follow me." We began to climb a net connected to a mast. I reached the top and sat down on one of the beams connected to the sails. After a few minutes, Ryker arrived.

"Hi," I said.

"Hi," Ryker replied," How did you climb that so fast?"

"Easily," I answered.

"Yeah, well I only have one arm."

"Oh my gosh! I forgot, I'm so sorry! Why didn't you say something?"

"I'm fine. But enough of that."

"What were you gonna give me?"

"Oh, right. This." Ryker put his hand in his pocket and pulled out a diamond that was maybe two inches across and neatly chiseled. I knew what it was the second I saw it.

"Ryker… that's… that's the diamond from Lost Island. How did you…"

"I found it before the eruption. Here, take it."

"Oh my goodness. I don't know what to say," I gasped, taking the diamond.

"You don't have to say anything. You deserve this," Ryker said.

"No, I can't take this. You should…"

"I don't want it," Ryker said as he pushed my hand back. "You deserve it. You're the heir. Please, just take it. I insist."

"Well, okay then," I conceded. "If you insist."

"I just wanted you to have it because you're amazing and I love you. I don't think any boy could possibly deserve a girl like you. I'm just hoping I might be close enough."

"Close enough?" I asked. "Close enough? Is that really what you think of yourself? Ryker, you are more than enough. How have you not figured that out yet?"

"Well, no one ever told me I was good enough when I was younger," Ryker answered.

"You'll always be good enough," I said. The look in Ryker's eyes suddenly changed, and he smiled. But his smile seemed more sincere this time, as though he had found something he had been looking for all of his life: someone else's approval.

All this time I had needed something from him, forgetting that he needed something from me. It was a bittersweet moment when I finally realized that I had been the first person to ever love him. And it was nice to know that he loved me in return.

I looked at the diamond in my hand and asked, "Ryker, did this voyage feel any different to you, different than all the other ones?"

"I guess so," Ryker said.

"I don't know why," I said. "I just feel changed."

"In what way?"

"I'm not sure. I guess I feel more confident, you know, like I finally did something with some worth to it."

"Yeah," Ryker agreed. "I mean, you're yourself again, but better."

"You know what?" I said. "All throughout our journey, even in despair, hope was never lost, just hidden, waiting to be found again."

"You know what *is* lost?" Ryker asked.

"What?"

"Sawyer's sanity," Ryker grinned. "Along with Alice's, Sydney's and Donna's."

"Donna never had any sanity."

"True."

"And I guess I'm a little insane, myself, sometimes," I joked.

"No, you're just very, very emotional."

"Yeah," I said. "Let's just go with that."

"Oh, look," Ryker said, looking into the harbor. "The psychopaths are back."

"I guess we'd better get down there before everyone starts teasing us," I said as I stood up. "Are you able to climb down with your arm the way it is?"

"Yeah, I'm fine," Ryker answered, standing up. "But wait. Don't go. Not yet."

"Oh…" I turned towards him. "Why? Is something wrong?"

"Nothing's wrong," Ryker said. "I just… I mean, everything is settled down a little now, and Sawyer's not here to make fun of us, and…"

"What is it?"

"I don't know, I just…"

"Ryker, spit it out."

"I…"

"Use your mouth," I suggested.

Ryker was speechless. He didn't know what to say, and I didn't either. We could both tell something was about to happen, but neither of us knew what. As I gazed into Ryker's eyes, everything fell silent.

I stepped closer to him, realizing what was going on now. And at that moment, I remembered the first time I ever saw his face. I remembered the feeling that I couldn't comprehend that day. It was the same feeling that I felt now. Everything seemed to strangely fall into place. Everything seemed perfect. Suddenly, all of my wits left, as Ryker kissed me.

Of course, I began to cry. The moment was too perfect to handle. I didn't know why I was crying, because I was extremely happy.

"You okay?" Ryker asked as he took my hands.

"Absolutely perfect," I answered with a nod.

"Yeah, me too," Ryker grinned.

"Well, that's just great," Sawyer chimed in from the top of the net. "But now I'm getting bored. I saw the kissing... now, that was some good..."

"Please don't," I begged.

"Oh, Sawyer, we can always count on you to ruin the moment," Ryker said.

"Oh, Ryker, we can always count on you to ditch your friends for some overrated girl," Sawyer said.

"Overrated! I saved your life!" I scolded.

"Did not," Sawyer argued.

"Would you have rather drowned the night we met?" I asked.

"Belle, can you get down here?" Sydney yelled up and then said, "Alice, you can open your eyes now. They're done."

"Oh good!" Alice said with a sigh," You two love birds may have liked it, but I did not enjoy your little smooch-fest."

"*Squawk!* Smooch-fest!" Donna chirped.

"We weren't smooching!" I yelled down.

"The whole concept is just gross! Please, next time, smooch where others don't have to see you!" Alice complained.

"We weren't smooching," Ryker yelled. "It was just one kiss. That was all that happened."

"Yeah, and then Belle started crying like she does every ten minutes," Sawyer said.

"I do not cry every ten minutes!" I denied hotly.

"No, just a lot," Ryker said. "But we should probably get going."

"I'm surprised she didn't cry into your shoulder!" Sawyer teased.

"Oh, be quiet," I hushed him as we climbed down the net onto the deck.

"Well, where are we gonna go?" Sydney asked.

"On another voyage," I said.

"Can we pick an easier one?" Ryker asked. "I didn't really enjoy falling into a volcano, busting my head open, breaking my arm, and breaking my ribs all in one day."

"Oh, so now you mention all of the times we got hurt," I observed.

"I didn't say I was upset we went," Ryker said.

"Oh, none of us are upset," I said. "I got this nice diamond, and a hat that actually fits, and some gold."

"You got the diamond!" Sydney squealed.

"Yeah, Ryker found it before the eruption," I said.

"Ryker, how could you?" Sawyer griped.
"How could I what?" Ryker asked.

"You found the diamond and you gave it away, to your girlfriend! That's what happens when you get all lovey-dovey and stupid!" Sawyer fussed.

"How selfish!" Alice chimed in.

"It's not selfish, it's selfless," I argued. "Because that's just the kind of person Ryker is, and I…"

"Can we please get back on topic?" Sydney interrupted.

"Yeah, sure," I agreed, as I climbed on top of the table, stood up, and clapped my hands to get the crew's attention.

"Well, everyone, we have successfully made it into and out of Lost Island alive, with the sacred treasure. This diamond in my hand is the priceless diamond of Pedro Francisco. And yes, I may be the one that holds it in my hand, but we are all heirs. We all did this together, no one less than another. And as heirs, we will hold ourselves to the highest standards, because we are not just kids.

"We are heroes! And if any of you can't see that, open your eyes. And on this next voyage, and the one after, and the one after that, we will have courage, and we will never give up. Who's with me?"

The Stowaways cheered with excitement.

"Well then let us set sail! Another voyage awaits!" I declared. "Sydney, get us a map. Sawyer, Alice, hoist the sails! I'll get the anchor."

"And what about me?" Ryker asked.

"Well, you're pretty beat up, and you've done a lot for us lately. You can take a break," I answered.

"Oh, sure! He gets a break! He's your favorite!" Sawyer complained.

"Get to work, Sawyer," I ordered.

"Belle! I found a map!" Sydney exclaimed.

"Great!" I finished lifting the anchor. "Okay, everyone! Come over here!"

Everyone gathered around in a circle.

"Alright, guys. We are about to depart from the harbor, and once we do, our voyage will be completely over, and we'll be going on a new one," I said. "Okay, hands in the middle. 'Aye,' on three."

"*Squawk!* I have no hands. I am handless," Donna chirped.

"Just put in your wing," Alice said.

Everyone put their hand (or wing) in and shouted, "One, two, three, Aye!"

And with that our voyage ended. We set sail for a new adventure, ready to take on anything, knowing that we would press on till the end so long as there was breath in our lungs and hope in the backs of our minds. The Legend of Lost Island never died, but lived on in the hearts of the Stowaways, the heirs of Pedro Francisco.

The End

Coming Soon from

Grace Under Pressure Publishing

The Return of the Cobra

by

Eliza Crooks

the exciting sequel to

The Voyage of the Pegasus

by

Eliza Crooks

Visit graceunderpressure.com for more information.

www.ingramcontent.com/pod-product-compliance
Lightning Source LLC
Chambersburg PA
CBHW072353110726
47909CB00003B/687